The World That Could Be

The City Rises by Umberto Boccioni. 1910.

The World That Could Be

Robert C. North

W · W · NORTON & COMPANY
New York · London

W. W. Norton & Company, Inc., 500 Fifth Avenue, New York, N.Y. 10110

This book was published originally as a part of THE PORTABLE STANFORD, a series of books published by the Stanford Alumni Association, Stanford, California. This edition first published by W. W. Norton & Company, Inc. in 1978 by arrangement with the Stanford Alumni Association.

Library of Congress Cataloging in Publication Data
North, Robert Carver.
The world that could be.
Reprint of the ed. published by Stanford
Alumni Association, Stanford, Calif., in series:
The Portable Stanford.
1. Utopias. 2. Computers and civilization.
I. Title.
HX806.N68 1978 321'.07 77-25071
ISBN 0-393-05677-5
ISBN 0-393-00882-7 pbk.

4 5 6 7 8 9 0

For Robin

FOREWORD

This book is the outgrowth of four preoccupations of mine over the past two decades. During the mid-1950s I became increasingly dissatisfied with traditional explanations of international competitions, crises, and war, but the causes of my uneasiness were elusive. Then, in the August 1957 issue of *Harper's*, I read an article by Peter Drucker entitled "The New Philosophy Comes to Life," which cited two books and an article that deserved careful scrutiny. The books were *What Is Life?* by physicist Erwin Schrödinger and *The Image* by economist Kenneth Boulding. The article, written by biologist Ludwig von Bertalanffy, was an early draft of his subsequent book, *General System Theory.* These writings distinguished, and tried to define relations between, the wholes and the component parts of organizations as well as of organisms. They focused my attention on rates of growth and decline, and on amounts and levels of phenomena such as population, technology, resources, territory, production, consumption, machinery, weapons, education, health facilities, wartime casualties, and the like. They drew attention to ratios, patterns, and trends in the allocation of resources, goods, services, benefits, and costs. The writings of these three men suggested to me that many words—liberty, freedom, equity, justice, welfare, war, peace, progress, and the like—were not likely to mean much beyond rhetoric unless they could be linked in specific ways to such issues as population growth, the purposes to which advances in technology are applied, the criteria by which resources are allocated, and trade-offs between today's demands and tomorrow's safeguards.

Secondly, in response to my reading of such materials, I began looking at human beings in terms of their anthropological background. Initially, I was influenced by Elman Service's book, *Primitive Social Organization: An Evolutionary Approach*, which offered an explanation of how prehistoric institutional forms prepared the way for the emergence of the state. Subsequently, I read *Stone Age Economics*, by Marshall Sahlins, which seemed to place human beings and their acquisition, exchange, and allocation of goods in a new and revealing perspective. Against this deep prehistoric background it became evident to me that the events and relationships of today—or of any historical era—are but brief data points in the long, sweeping curves of human development. Thus if we focus only on a few of these points, we may miss some of the persisting dynamics of the past that are generating our thrust through the present and into the future.

A third source of concepts and data for this book has been an ongoing, computerized research project—strongly influenced by my reading of Schrödinger, von Bertalanffy, Boulding, and others—which has used population, resources, and technology, as well as various allocation ratios and so forth, in an effort to obtain new insights into the behavior of states and empires. A major development within this project, undertaken in collaboration with Professor Nazli Choucri of MIT, has been the development of simulation and forecasting techniques as an approach to the construction of future alternatives. Early phases of this research were funded by the Ford Foundation. The National Science Foundation has supported more recent phases.

Finally, this book is also an outgrowth of my personal concern that the demographic, social, economic, and political systems (of which all of us are constituent parts) have already spun beyond our control and thus threaten our survival unless we can bend them to our rational will within the next few decades. The deep irony of the threat is that we ourselves, in the daily pursuit of our more immediate and narrow interests, contribute to its perpetuation and growth. This tendency, in my view, cuts across most boundaries of class, culture, ideology, and national interest so that, directly or indirectly, virtually all of us contribute to it. The only way out may depend upon our ability to see more clearly what we are doing to ourselves and to our descendants.

Against this background, my overriding concern in this book is not to advocate any particular policy or program, but to press for new insights, expanded horizons, the acceleration of social learning, and concerted efforts toward the widening of perceived alternatives.

In thinking about these problems over the years, as well as in the writing of this book, I have been influenced by a large number of students, colleagues, and friends—more than can be mentioned here. I am particularly indebted, however, to the late Harold Fisher, to Easton Rothwell, Thomas Milburn, Paul Bernstein, Andrew Willard, Matthew Willard, Joshua Goldstein, Loren Bloch, Peter Corning, Kent Smith, Lawrence Ng, Pierre Noyes, Robert Brownstein, Rudolf Moos, Paul Ekman, and Nazli Choucri; to my colleagues in the "Prospects for Survival" seminar at Stanford University—Malcolm McWhorter, Kenneth Cooper, and Bruce Lusignan; and to our students in that class.

For continuing editorial advice and the selection of the artwork, I am deeply grateful to Cynthia Fry Gunn.

Stanford, California

Robert C. North

ILLUSTRATIONS

TABLE OF CONTENTS

Marble idol found at Naxos.

CHAPTER ONE

SHAPING THE FUTURE

BOOKSTORES TODAY CARRY HUNDREDS of publications about current human crises and disturbing problems of the future. Some are pessimistic, spreading gloom and predicting doom. "The future of mankind is at stake," according to many. Others are optimistic, reassuring us that technology will save mankind or that some other solution will turn up.

How about you? Are you an optimist or a pessimist? Do you believe that every day in every way the world is getting better and better? Worse and worse? Six of one and half a dozen of the other? Do you believe in progress? Or that the world is retrogressive, rapidly becoming unraveled? If you believe the latter, there is much to support your viewpoint—energy shortages, taxes, inflation, unemployment, crime in the streets, urban decay, population problems, arms races, monetary crises, and the possibility of nuclear war, to mention only a few. According to economist Robert Heilbroner in his book *An Inquiry into the Human Prospect*, "The outlook is for what we may call 'convulsive change'—change forced upon us by external events rather than by conscious choice, by catastrophe rather than by calculation." Or do you think that the problems can be solved if we just build nuclear reactors, develop better access to solar energy, throw the bad guys out of office, reinvigorate capitalism, establish socialism, increase our military capabilities, or disarm?

What you think about the world and its future may depend upon your view of human nature. Do you view people as innately selfish, competitive, aggressive, and violent—incapable of transforming themselves into something better? Or are people, though often greedy and corruptible, also capable of great generosity, integrity, and noble undertaking? Though sometimes stupid or slavish to habit, do they also have an extraordinary capacity for insight, vision, and invention? Have the great deeds of history been wrought by the rare saint, genius, or prophet? Or is human progress largely fashioned from the day-to-day decisions and harsh experiences of common men and women? Consider Heilbroner's view: "There seems no hope for rapid changes in the human character traits that would have to be modified to bring about a peaceful, organized reorientation of life styles. Men and women, much as they are today, will set the pace and determine the necessary means for the social changes that will eventually have to be made." Are you ready to take on this responsibility?

What do *you* think of the human prospect? Perhaps you see the men and women of the world divided into good guys and bad guys, the enlightened and the unenlightened, heroes and villains, Christians and heathens, Moslems and infidels, progressives and reactionaries (or conservatives and radicals)—locked in a struggle for dominance. Perhaps you agree with Heilbroner's assessment that "no capitalist nation has yet imagined the extent of the alterations it must undergo to attain a viable stationary socioeconomic structure." If you agree with Heilbroner that capitalism is part of the problem, you might also think about his further conviction that "no socialist state has evidenced the needed willingness to subordinate the national interests to supranational ones." Or, if you come from a Third World country that aspires to catch up with the West, you might ponder his conclusion that "no developing country has fully confronted the implications of becoming a 'modern' nation-state whose industrial development must be severely limited, or considered the strategy for such a state in a world in which the Western nations, capitalist and socialist both, will continue for a long period to enjoy the material advantages of their early start."

Paradoxically, among writers, some of the more optimistic seem to view human nature as fundamentally unchangeable (therefore, it is useless, if not dysfunctional, to interfere in what is viewed as a natural course of events), whereas some of the more pessimistic exhort readers, statesmen, and the public at large to do *something*—recycle, establish communes, dissolve the oil companies, reduce economic or population growth to zero, or abolish capitalism. Are you an "interventionist," pessimistic about the present but insistent that there must be a better way? Or are you inclined toward a laissez-faire policy, convinced that many of our difficulties have been brought about, in fact, by bleeding-heart interventionists tinkering with the Constitution? According to Heilbroner, "The drift toward the strong exercise of political power—a movement given its initial momentum by the need to exercise a much wider and deeper administration of both production and consumption —is likely to attain added support from the psychological insecurity that will be sharpened in a period of unrest and uncertainty."

At least the more adamant of the laissez-faire advocates have solutions that are relatively specific. Go back to the old ways, they say, free up the marketplace, put an end to all this welfare nonsense, stop coddling criminals, and our problems will begin to straighten out. Some of the more radical interventionists also have solutions—get rid of the capitalists, they tell us, and all will be well. With few exceptions the hard-core purveyors of doom and gloom, on the other hand, while issuing dire predictions about the future and offering a favorite panacea, present little else that is genuinely futuristic. Few, if any, concrete solutions are offered; seldom, if ever, is it made explicit how the favorite panacea will alter the course of affairs; and rarely is a practical course of action proposed, however crude, for cleaning up the mess they say we are in.

Agreeing on the condition of the world around them, the interventionists are by no means in universal accord about what should be done. In an essay entitled "The Case Against Helping the Poor" (*Psychology Today*, September 1974), biologist Garrett Hardin asserts that with the continued dwindling of the world's resources, the differences in prosperity between the rich and the poor can only increase. The stake is survival. Should the well-fed people feed the starving? Are the rich responsible for all the rest of humanity? Many critics of aid and welfare programs think not. But since we all share life on this planet, Hardin declares, "no single person or institution has the right to destroy, waste, or use more than a fair share of its resources." He then proceeds with a provocative argument.

Metaphorically each rich nation can be seen as a lifeboat full of comparatively rich people. In the ocean outside the lifeboat swim the poor of the world, who would like to get in. So here we sit, with say 50 people in our lifeboat, while 100 others thrash about in the water outside, begging to be brought aboard—or at least to be thrown a life jacket. What should the lifeboat passengers do? To be generous, argues Hardin, let us assume that there is room for ten more in the boat, making a total capacity of 60. But out of the 100 people struggling against the ocean, how can ten be fairly chosen for rescue; and once aboard, would not their additional weight destroy the margin of safety enjoyed by the 50 as long as the boat is not fully loaded?

Others take a similar viewpoint. The survival of mankind, they argue, depends upon the maintenance of an island of plenty in what amounts to a vast sea of deprivation. Someone must maintain such an island in order to protect the material and intellectual seed grain for the future. Of all places on earth, the United States comes closest to representing an island of plenty; hence we in this country owe its protection and survival not only to our children but to all generations to come.

Why Read This Book?

What about this book—where does it fit in? Does it spread more doom and gloom or is it optimistic? Are there solutions in it? Does it advocate more free enterprise, more government controls, or possibly some form of totalitarianism? Where does it stand on Arab oil and nuclear reactors? Is there any good reason why you should read it?

The perspective of this book is that no answers are evident because they are locked up in you and me and in the minds, hearts, dispositions, and habit patterns of everyone else in the world as well. In ways that will become more explicit further along, we all help determine the shape of tomorrow, next year, and the turn of the century by what we have done (or have failed to do) in the past, by what we are doing now, and by what we do in our own homely ways tomorrow and thereafter, day by day, for as long as we live. It is therefore the purpose of this book not to provide solutions, which it cannot do, but to shock you into some fresh perspectives, to make you angry enough to think about the world and its people in new ways, and to identify some tools that might enable us all to participate in the generation of alternate futures.

Six Basic Assumptions

In carrying out this purpose, we shall proceed from the following six assumptions:

1. Human affairs are not solely, or even primarily, the outcome of economic or other material factors, but neither are they uniquely the result of "free will" or other intellectual, psychological, or spiritual forces. The course of events stems from the intense interaction of both types of influence. Thus, a change in any one important factor is likely to bring about changes in others. But human considerations can effect their own kind of *social determinism*: decisions of the past may limit today's options just as deeply embedded customs and institutions may blind us to promising alternatives.

2. Numbers are not "inhuman," but are closely intertwined with the way we live. They influence our values, just as our beliefs, preferences,

I Saw the Figure 5 in Gold by Charles Demuth. 1928.

and aspirations affect the numbers of people and things we deal with. Large numbers of people and things tend to widen and complicate the scope of our moral responsibility. We cannot confront the future effectively unless we understand the connection between values and numbers, between the quantitative and the qualitative.

3. Our ability to cope successfully with the critical problems of the future will depend a great deal upon both the potential and the limitations of human nature. But what we commonly refer to as "human nature" is not fixed and immutable. To a large extent each individual human being *is* what he or she *does*, and over the millennia people's activities have changed enormously. Our predispositions and traits have undergone many changes as alterations have come about in our relations with the physical environment and with each other.

4. Although human beings have achieved progress in some dimensions, we cannot assume that they have progressed in all dimensions, or even in a few of the more important ones. Through the ages people have vastly increased their ability to harness mechanical energy and transform the products of the earth for their special purposes. We have also found ways of maiming and killing each other in greater and greater numbers. It is not at all clear that we have made much moral or ethical progress overall. Progress in one dimension often contributes to retrogression in another.

5. Although each human event is unique and people's ways of doing things are constantly changing, certain general tendencies and broad patterns of behavior have been repeated again and again throughout our prehistory and history. An important key to coping with the future involves an ability to distinguish between what is recurring and what is unique. In order to achieve a perspective of what our possibilities for the future are, we need to review some patterns of the past—not only the relatively recent past, but also the dim past which includes the beginnings of human affairs.

6. The individual is shaped in large part by his or her society, but the society is the outcome of its individual human components. Neither can be understood properly without an understanding of the other. In dealing with the future, then, we should not focus primarily upon the individual, nor primarily upon the society, but upon the dynamic interactions between the two.

One approach to the future advocated in this book involves the building of utopias—not just one or two, but perhaps hundreds or even thousands. You may object that utopia building is a softheaded, imbecilic pastime, a kind of withdrawal from the real world, as useless as daydreaming, although it may be reassuring to learn that at least one utopia influenced the shaping of the United States Constitution. The construction of utopias can help us broaden our perspectives and evaluate alternatives before we commit ourselves to an irrevocable course of action.

The Meaning and Usefulness of Utopias

The word *utopia*, coined from the Greek, means "nowhere." It was first used in the sixteenth century by Sir Thomas More in his book *Utopia* as the name of an island, a figment of his imagination, where an ideal commonwealth was said to exist. According to dictionary definitions, a utopia refers to an imaginary country with ideal laws and social conditions, or to an impractical and usually impossibly ideal scheme for social, political, or economic improvement. More broadly, the German sociologist Karl Mannheim, author of *Ideology and Utopia*, writes that the term "may be applied to any process of thought which receives its impetus not from the direct force of social reality but from concepts, such as symbols, fantasies, dreams, ideas, and the like, which in the most comprehensive sense of that term are nonexistent."

Although the concept of utopia has become firmly associated with Sir Thomas More, the genre made its appearance long before his time. Indeed, it was Plato's *Republic* that provided the general model to which all subsequent fictions have been indebted. Unlike radical reformers of a later day, however, Plato was not proposing an ideal commonwealth that might be brought into existence overnight, by repeating some catch phrases and making a few sweeping changes in the social, political, or economic institutions. Plato's ideal was a counsel of perfection. Ages might be required to bring his envisaged state into being. The purpose of Plato's utopia building, according to Mannheim, was primarily to construct an authoritarian design that would "buttress, in as rational terms as possible, a static and hierarchically ordered political system."

The utopian writings of More and his fellow humanists during the Renaissance, by contrast, were the expression, according to Mannheim, of a powerful "wave of intellectual and social release"—a radical challenge to the more traditional ideas and rigid institutions of the time. A staunch Catholic who suffered execution rather than submit to the demands made upon him by Henry VIII, More was concerned with a revolution that would be much deeper than a mere change in the form of government or even a shift of power from one economic class to another. The only true revolution, he believed, is moral, and hence a change in a society's institutions will be of limited value unless the new arrangement produces good men and good women. His *Utopia* was thus an attempt to infuse a concrete social system with Christian ethical values.

More's criticism of contemporary institutions and the communism of his Utopians have made his book popular with many modern revolutionaries, who have viewed it as a document of social protest. But More himself, unlike many "true believers" before and since, expressed reservations about his own creation. "I admit that not a few things in the manners and laws of the Utopians seemed very absurd to me," he wrote in the last paragraphs of the book, "their way of waging war, their religious customs, as well as other matters, but especially the keystone of their entire system, namely, their communal living without the use of money. . . . Yet I must confess that there are many things in the Utopian Commonwealth that I wish rather than expect to see followed among our citizens." Drawing upon his own travels, as well as his humanistic studies, political theorist James Harrington during the Cromwellian regime used a comparative study of constitutions as a means of identifying that form of government most ideally suited to England. The most realistic of the humanist utopias, Harrington's *The Commonwealth of Oceana* (1656), subsequently exerted a notable influence on makers of the United States Constitution. In *The New Atlantis* Sir Francis Bacon expressed an aggressive faith in science and its liberating role.

During the eighteenth and early nineteenth centuries the widespread social unrest engendered by the industrial revolution as well as the consequent economic and political readjustments of the time found expression in a succession of somewhat heterogeneous utopias modeled on the work of the earlier humanists. The literary utopias constructed in the decades following the French Revolution were directed more consistently toward a single political ideal. Among them were those of the so-called utopian socialists, such as Saint-Simon, Babeuf, Fourier, and Owen. With variations in individual perspective, these writers believed that unemployment and other undesirable outcomes of the industrial revolution could be eliminated and the economic security of the masses achieved by means of rational planning, through social ownership of the means of production. Moreover, much to the subsequent irritation of Karl Marx and his disciples, these early-nineteenth-century utopia builders thought that propertied groups could be persuaded to surrender their holdings peacefully and even voluntarily.

Specifically, Marx's collaborator, Friedrich Engels, criticized the anti-bourgeois but idealistic utopians for trying to "evolve out of the human brain" the solution of social problems that lay "hidden in undeveloped social conditions." As a consequence, Engels argued, these new social systems were foredoomed: "The more completely they were worked out in detail, the more they could not help drifting into pure fantasies." Engels rebuked them, Mannheim writes, for perpetuating the "sentimental delusions of the eighteenth-century *Philosophes*, who naively fancied that they could bring their fellow men to carry through a reorganization of society merely by placing before them certain abstract ideals." The place to start was with the proletariat, the only class which, in Marxian terms, could bring about a true reorganization of society.

Many utopia builders of the nineteenth century went beyond pen-and-ink creations and created real-life communities. Centered chiefly in the United States, both religious and nonreligious groups established large numbers of model settlements—most of them self-consciously experimental and usually communistic. Among the more notable of these attempts were the Shaker, Hutterite, Zoarite, Owenite, Fourierist, and Perfectionist settlements. Such experimental communities appeared in New England, New York, the Middle West, including Texas, and in various other far-flung localities. The communism of the religious societies was often thoroughgoing. Incoming members normally turned over all property to a common fund. No wages were paid, and every effort was made to ensure that no one in such a community was either rich or poor. Every individual was guaranteed the necessities of life and care in sickness and old age.

In some societies the emphasis was upon eugenics as well as economics. Influenced by Charles Darwin's *The Origin of Species*, the Oneida Community tried to perfect human society by the "scientific" arrangement of sexual unions. Since human beings were perceived as shaped by a combination of heredity and environment, the community hoped to influence the values, moral character, and behavior of future generations by the careful selection of their parents as well as by the molding of the society in which they would live.

Retrospectively, we see how the utopians have often been dismissed as impractical dreamers. Pen-and-ink utopias, such as those of More, Harrington, Bacon, and others, bore little resemblance to reality and had no possibility of being tested. The model communities, on the other hand, could not be effectively tested unless they could be separated from the larger, encompassing society—and despite their most heroic efforts, that was seldom economically, politically, or even socially feasible.

In modern times, the possibility of subjecting experimental, real-life communities to rigorous test through isolation from the encompassing society seems even more remote than in the nineteenth century. Then, at least, settlements could be established on the frontier and a certain degree of independence maintained until the larger society encompassed them. Now, in the latter decades of the twentieth century, there are virtually no frontiers left—none, at least, that cannot be penetrated economically and politically.

The usefulness of pen-and-ink, or purely conceptual, utopias, on the

Rock painting of human figures from Sebaaieni Cave.

other hand, has been greatly enhanced by the development of computer modeling techniques and other specialized methodologies that make it possible to generate hundreds or even thousands of alternate societies —and then pick and choose among them as we wish. Today, a variety of attempts are already underway, with the aid of computers, to create new utopias designed to help us plan for the future.

Many people object to the idea of trying to model a society. They point out, rightly, that any such attempt is certain to be a gross oversimplification of real life. Even worse, it is likely to overlook the subtle complexity of thought and feeling—as if human beings were themselves machines, no better than electronic computers. Moreover, the major "planned" societies that have been established in the real world—the

USSR, for example, or the People's Republic of China—are seen by many as having degraded, even brutalized, people rather than setting them free.

These are important objections, and they need to be taken seriously. But they overlook one fundamental consideration. Each of us carries around in his or her head a "model" of the world, of society, of the local community, of the family—even of oneself—and none of us can deal with any of these entities, even superficially, without reference to the appropriate mental construct or model. It is the only way we have of relating to other people and to our larger surroundings. We draw upon these models whenever we discuss affairs, whenever we vote, and whenever we plan for the future in any way. Such models affect our moral values and choices. In considering possible alternatives, therefore, the central questions are what models are we carrying about and using, what are their implications, and what do we want them to mean for ourselves, our children, and others?

Usually, we know very little about the models we actually use because we do not think about them often. Even when we do think about them, however, we normally ignore the assumptions about people that underlie them, and also the outcomes for ourselves and others that may emerge from them. Any social, economic, or political planning, any policymaking, and any effort to develop future alternatives should therefore begin with a discussion of our basic assumptions about people.

The early chapters of this book will consider how human beings have lived at different stages of their prehistory and history. Subsequent chapters will deal with certain basic patterns of growth and change and will suggest how they have influenced the ways in which people have felt, thought, and acted. After that we will examine three models of society—a "tooth and claw" model, a "competitive-welfare" model, and an "equal-access" model—each predicated upon its own assumptions and each generating its own implications for human affairs today and in the future. Depending upon your personal views about our human limitations and potentials, you will probably be inclined toward one or another of these three models. Much more important, however, is the possibility that these grossly oversimplified models may break us out of our narrow, habitual modes of thinking and help us to identify wholly new ways of organizing ourselves, making a living, distributing goods, controlling crime, and resolving conflicts. Through the innovative use of such models we may discover that we can now shape the future more consciously than in the past, as an outcome of our personal day-to-day choices and activities.

Summit of a limestone stele at Susa.

CHAPTER TWO

THE GREAT SWEEP OF HUMAN EXPERIENCE

PEOPLE ARE SUCH DIVERSE and complex creatures that we are often at a loss to identify what "human nature" really is or to be certain whether or not it even exists. As soon as we try to generalize, someone is sure to remind us of all the physical, cultural, intellectual, emotional, and other differences that characterize people in various parts of the world today—let alone throughout the great sweep of human prehistory and history. One way to get at this problem is to try to identify those characteristics and dispositions that all people in all times and places seem to have had in common.

Every person requires at the very minimum such basic resources as air, food, water, and some amount of territory. To stay alive, every human being must ingest energy in some form from the environment. And this requires sustained access to critical resources. From these naive propositions we can infer that the larger a given population, the greater will be the amount of resources demanded.

Technology and the Availability of Resources

The availability of the resources that people use is determined first of all by the natural distribution of those resources on the planet. But availability also depends upon the levels and characteristics of human technology—people's knowledge and skills. Technology develops as an outcome of the ability of human beings to interact with the environment as well as with each other, to learn from their experiences, and to organize their knowledge and skills in new ways in order to achieve certain purposes. Thus defined, technology encompasses all aspects of human knowledge and skills from early Stone Age techniques of hunting and gathering to modern agriculture, commerce, or industry. Mathematics is a form of technology, as are the knowledge and skills applied in social organizations, politics, economics, and the arts and humanities. Tools serve as crude indicators of a people's technology. In a rough way we may thus obtain some idea of how people lived in the past by examining the tools they used and the products they fabricated: flint scrapers and arrowheads found in a grave site suggest a Stone Age level of knowledge and skills, whereas an electronic computer or a nuclear reactor would be characteristic of latter twentieth-century technology.

From as far back as we have evidence of human life, people have used their knowledge and skills in order to improve their access to resources with the hope of satisfying their demands. Advances in technology may make available a resource that was previously out of reach, or may provide uses for resources which were previously perceived as unusable. Resource scarcities are therefore not constant, but depend upon human knowledge and skills and the effort and expense involved in acquiring the materials that are in demand. The access people have to critical resources may also be affected drastically by prevailing social, economic, and political institutions.

Technology and the Demand for Resources

Technology itself creates its own demand for resources. A primitive axe requires only a stone head, a haft, some sinews, and the biological energy of the craftsman who gathers the components and binds them together. A sailing ship requires more resources, and an electronic computer still vastly more. Applications of technology commonly require three types of resources: 1) either muscular or mechanical energy to provide a driving force (to shape the tool or to use it); 2) structural materials from which the tool, instrument, weapon, machine, factory, or reactor is fashioned; and 3) the fibers, minerals, and other materials that are mined or processed in order to feed, clothe, house, or otherwise serve some human population. Thus, the more advanced the level of technology among a given population, the greater will be the range and quantity of resources needed to sustain that technology and advance it further.

An advancing technology may also alter a people's perception of what they "need." Consequently their demands are likely to increase.

The needs of human beings during the Paleolithic Age, for example, were quite limited compared with the vast and complicated needs commonly identified by people today. We can learn something about ourselves by making a list of our "necessities." Changes in technology not only bring about alterations in our values, they also affect our beliefs, habits, and customs; our social, political, economic, and educational institutions; and our expectations of the future. In terms of their ability to change our lives and perhaps even our innermost "nature," the world's great revolutionaries have been inventors and innovators rather than militant politicians or soldiers.

The application of technology, like biological metabolism, depends upon complex energy transformation chains, portions of them man-made, reaching back to the earth itself and ultimately to the sun. Each such energy transformation, like each transfer in a food chain, involves some amount of degradation from an available, concentrated form to an unavailable, dispersed form. This inescapable degradation in the usefulness of energy contributes to the depletion of resources and to pollution. These are not new phenomena: even ancient societies often depleted the game supply, wore out the soil, started forest fires, contaminated streams, and the like. But we may expect the possibilities for depletion and pollution to increase with greater numbers of people and with more extensive and advanced technologies.

Our early forebears had to make whatever uses they could of energy-rich materials as they came to hand. Hunters and gatherers of the Paleolithic Age depended on game and whatever useful plants happened to grow in their particular locale. They had to mobilize all the technology they possessed in order to survive the vicissitudes of nature. But the subsequent course of human development has been characterized by a growing capacity to harness mechanical energy and other natural forces in order to control and alter the environment.

For millennia people had to use their own muscles or those of slaves or beasts of burden. In low-energy societies there was little surplus for community innovations or other complex organizational activities. Whatever energy was available had to be used for mere survival. The substitution of mechanical energy for animal and muscle power made it increasingly feasible to tap resources of the earth that would otherwise be unreachable. Generally, however, it was not until the invention of the steam engine that the use of mechanical energy began to increase significantly. Other types of motive power were developed thereafter. With these changes in technology, the importance of the man-made factors of production, such as capital and skills, has increased relative to the natural productive forces of the earth.

None of this transformed energy has come free. At the very least a human being must expend some amount of his own energy in order to unlock and apply a greater amount of energy from the environment. More complex transformations have required the investment of considerable amounts of stored energy in order to generate even larger amounts of applicable energy and to maintain it ready for use. Accordingly, each transformation and application of energy has tended to exact a toll upon the environment.

Some advances in technology have yielded greater economies in the transfer and utilization of primary energy, that is, greater utility of output is achieved for each unit of resource input. (The efficiency of a machine is the ratio of the mechanical work done *by* the machine to the work done *on* the machine.) Overall, however, each major development in technology has tended to catalyze innumerable others—each requiring resources whether for structure (machines, tools, plant equipment), fuel (wood, coal, oil), or processing (wool, cotton, iron ore, and the like). So demands for resources continue to skyrocket.

Social, economic, and political organizations are essential aspects of technology. But organizational forms have changed as the number of people has increased and as new ways have been found to obtain, process, and distribute resources. From Paleolithic band, to tribe, to chiefdom, and to state, each transformation in human organizational form has marked a new stage in technology and culture.

Every society functions within a particular physical environment which provides the resources utilized by its economy. The demand for resources will be influenced by the size of the population, the level and characteristics of the technology, and the values of the people. The availability of resources depends, in turn, not only upon their geographical distribution, but also upon the technological, organizational, and fiscal capabilities that the society has developed. But all these factors tend to be intensely interactive: each affects the others, and each is likely to be influenced by any change among the others.

Five Revolutionary System Breaks

The course of human development seems to be marked by five great "system breaks" or revolutions of technology. Each of these has involved a transformation in the way people have perceived the universe, their assumptions about their relationship to it, the values that have been professed and/or invoked, and the ways in which people have expected to relate to one another. Indeed, we can almost imagine "human nature" itself undergoing significant modifications during each of these great technological revolutions. As new views have developed, people have discovered different ways of ordering their values and defining their self-interest, and these changes have then affected their future actions.

The first of these system breaks presumably took place when our remote ancestors learned to make stone tools in the early Paleolithic Age. The second was marked by human control over fire. The third, often referred to as the Neolithic revolution, involved a transformation from hunting and gathering as the prevailing technology to the mastery of agriculture by societies in many parts of the world.

Later, the change from agriculture to industry amounted to another major system break, a fourth massive "revolution" of technological, economic, and political components that began in the late eighteenth century and has lasted down to the present. And today we confront a fifth system break, the computer revolution—the transition from industry as the prevailing technology to cybernation—which is almost certain to involve a rapid and epic revolution in technological, economic, political, and social dimensions that will transform the ways people live throughout the world. Derived from the Greek word for steering, cybernation refers to the ways in which living organisms, as well as some machines, operate to close the gap between *what is* or *can be* and *what is preferred* or *ought to be*.

A vast amount of time has been required for these great revolutions to take place, although it is important to note that developments have accelerated greatly with each one. Prior to and even during the Neolithic revolution, the wisdom of the grandparent was instructive for children and grandchildren. But after the industrial revolution, and even more with the beginnings of cybernetics, the wisdom of yesterday is already under challenge today.

If the whole course of human prehistory and history is considered, it probably took our forebears some millions of years—until about 750,000 years ago or somewhat earlier—to make controlled use of fire. Similarly, our ancestors required almost four million years to replace hunting and gathering with agriculture, a gradual transition that began in Southeast Asia, the Middle East, and parts of America and gradually spread outward.

Recently excavated sites and artifacts, subjected to carbon dating, reveal that man-like creatures have existed somewhere between three and four million years. These hunting and gathering ancestors of our primeval past account for more than 99 percent of all human time. By contrast, all our written history and most of what we refer to as "civilization" are outcomes of the last few thousand years of this extensive period—not much more than a tick of the clock of human development.

Bronze Age rock engraving (1000 B.C.–500 B.C.) from Bohuslan, Island of Gotland, Sweden.

Yet we usually proceed as if these millions of years of our upbringing had never taken place. And often we accord our remote forebears more condescension than honor.

If we examine what is known about the development of human beings since their emergence as a species, three overall trends stand out: 1) the growth in the number of people; 2) spectacular advances in technology (knowledge and skills); and 3) spiraling demands by people for energy in one form or another and for other resources.

According to a speculative guess, the world population of our early human ancestors may have comprised about 100,000 individuals. For the overwhelming part of the ensuing three or four million years we can only rely on further speculative guesses. Over most of these many generations, the number of people grew very slowly. The most authoritative estimates show limited increases in the world's population from 40,000 years ago until about the seventeenth century. At the beginning of the Christian era the population of the whole world has been estimated at about 250 million people—roughly comparable to the population of the USSR today. It required more than a millennium and a half after that for the world's population to double, reaching about 500 million by 1650. After that the growth curve took a sharp upward turn. By 1850, 200 years later, it had doubled to something more than a billion. The next doubling took about 80 years, and the doubling after that about 45 years. Viewed from a somewhat different perspective, some millions of years were required for human beings to achieve a population size of about one billion by 1850. The next billion was added in 80 years (1850-1930). The third billion came along in only 30 years (1930-60), and the next took only about 15 years (1960-75), when the population reached four billion. If this trend continues, the United Nations forecasts that the fifth billion will be added in just slightly more than a decade.

The overall advancement of human technology is even more difficult to estimate than the growth of human populations. But scholars who have tried to date human inventions, however tentatively, and to count them have constructed a technology "growth curve" that looks remarkably like the world population curve.

Over the long course of the Paleolithic Age, the changes in human populations and technologies were so gradual as to seem almost imperceptible. Even the agricultural revolution did not take place in a single surge or a brief crisis, but gradually, over thousands of years. It seems to have begun independently in such far-flung regions as Central America, the Middle East, and Southeast Asia. Estimates differ, but the first developments in agriculture may have taken place as much as

14,000 years ago, or even earlier when Ice Age glaciers began to melt. Remains of people who lived in Jordan and Israel about this time provide evidence of the transition from hunting and gathering to agriculture. They subsisted largely upon fish and gazelle, but they sometimes used flint sickles to cut grasses and wild wheat and may have relied on crude picks for the planting of barley and wheat. As the Neolithic Age progressed, people learned—as much as 750,000 years or so after their first control of fire—to smelt copper and lead.

Another 3,000 to 4,000 years passed before the first full urban communities developed in the Tigris-Euphrates Valley. The addition of tin to copper produced the full Bronze Age technology. What we refer to as civilization dates only from about 5,000 years ago. Yet human cultures had reached complex levels of development long before that.

Life in Paleolithic Bands

Throughout the greater part of human existence people have lived as hunters and gatherers in small, more or less "self-regulating" bands such as those characterizing the Paleolithic Age, which extended from earliest times until about 11,000 years ago. A band was often an extended family consisting of grandparents, parents, offspring, uncles, aunts, and cousins. Depending upon the physical environment and the availability of resources, such a group might sustain a population of anywhere from a score or so to 100 or 150 people.

The hunting and gathering band was normally bound together by kinship ties, dependencies, common interests in survival, and shared beliefs and rituals. Although typical of the Paleolithic Age, this basic form of organization has survived down to the present (or until the recent past) among bushmen of Australia, New Guinea, and elsewhere; various Pigmy peoples; and Indians and Eskimos in remote parts of the Americas, eastern Siberia, and Greenland. Indeed, it is by studying such surviving bands, as well as by excavating ancient campsites and burial grounds, that we can reconstruct the lives of our Paleolithic ancestors. In this connection, the recent "discovery" by outsiders of the Tasaday, a small and isolated enclave of Stone Age people living in the rain forests of Mindanao, has focused new attention upon the technology and sociopolitical organization that characterize human life at this stage.

In contrast to many historical and even contemporary views of human nature as inherently self-centered, competitive, aggressive, and societies as inevitably exploitative, our early Stone Age ancestors lived in communities that tended to be group-centered, egalitarian, nonhierarchical, self-regulating, and participatory. There were no economic or social classes and no vast accumulations of private or governmental wealth.

As in some extended family groups today, each adult male (and in some societies, each adult female as well) was a member of the "council of the whole" and was expected to take part in the discussion of all major issues. Most group decisions were the outcome of free discussion and the reaching of a consensus, or near consensus. Action was taken voluntarily and on the basis of unanimity. Despite the existence of headmen and shamans, or medicine men, no one was accountable to a higher executive or to a subordinate. Today, the Tasaday provide us with new evidence of Stone Age people living without hierarchies, inequality, destructive competition, or violent conflict.

Leadership in hunting and gathering societies emerged from personal traits rather than from accidents of birth, and it was advisory rather than executive. The typical headman achieved status through personal characteristics and the building of a following through personally established ties. Prestige was bestowed by the group, not exacted by force. Only on raids, during a hunt, or in a ceremony was absolute authority sometimes accorded to a ritual leader, and then voluntarily and only for a specific purpose.

In the seventeenth century, Thomas Hobbes described life among our early forebears as "solitary, poor, nasty, brutal and short." Other writers, including Jean-Jacques Rousseau, idealized the "noble savage" and his mode of living. No doubt the truth lay somewhere in between, but for the most part, as anthropologist Marshall Sahlins explains in his book *Stone Age Economics*, the life of hunters and gatherers may not have been as difficult as it appears from a modern perspective. Generally, our Paleolithic ancestors worked less than we do. According to Sahlins, studies of aboriginal groups in many diverse parts of the world indicate that not more than three to five hours a day were normally spent in food-gathering activities. Kalahari desert Bushmen, for example, work about two and a half days a week for six and a half hours per day for a total of about 15 hours a week. One man's hunting and gathering will support four or five people. (Sahlins estimated that about 65 percent worked only 36 percent of the time and the other 35 percent did not have to work at all.) Compared with most of us today, hunters and gatherers seem to have kept "bankers' hours."

We tend to think of our hunting and gathering ancestors as poor because they had so few material goods compared with us. But poverty is a subjective and relative concept: provided we have sufficient food, water, air to breathe, living space, and protection from the elements, we are "poor" only relative to someone else. As Sahlins notes, when we assert with respect to the Stone Age hunter and gatherer that his or her wants were "restricted," desires "restrained," or wealth "limited," we are imposing the value structure of our own industrial, high consumption society.

The concept of the "economic" man is essentially a bourgeois construct, to a large extent the outcome of the last few centuries of commercial development and the industrial revolution with their characteristic emphasis upon almost spiraling possibilities for material acquisition. Compared to us, the hunter of those distant times might qualify as an "uneconomic" man or woman—his acquisitive expectations having been so restricted compared with our own. The introspective modern householder, having suffered all his life tyrannies of a competitive affluence—of keeping up not only with his own expectations, but also with those of his neighbor, and still making ends meet—might well regard the Paleolithic hunter and gatherer as free. In these terms, Sahlins concludes, the extremely limited material possessions of our earliest forebears may be viewed as having relieved them of many cares, thus permitting them to enjoy life more fully. Systematic studies of hunting and gathering societies still in existence today show that although some of them have times of hunger, starvation is uncommon and almost never endemic as it has become in India and other underdeveloped, essentially agricultural regions of the contemporary world. The dietary intake of a hunter-gatherer was likely to be less than sumptuous, but it was normally sufficient.

The most fundamental values among hunters and gatherers were associated with the welfare and survival of the group, and sharing was a normal practice. Insofar as the group was committed socially to kin relationships, it was committed morally to generosity, reciprocity, and mutual aid. For the most part, individual members of hunting and gathering societies enjoyed equal access to whatever resources were available. People competed for status as the best hunter, fisherman, dancer, or moccasin maker, but not for economic advantage.

Roles and status among our Paleolithic ancestors were determined by age, sex, and temperament rather than by wealth or physical coercion. The rewards and costs of day-to-day existence were shared more evenly than not. Those who had more food shared with those who had less. When food was plentiful, the whole group ate well. In times of scarcity, everyone in the group ate less well. Individuals who were physically capable of obtaining food could do so, since there were no artificial social or economic barriers between them and the basic resources, and weaker members were normally provided for. In times of severe starvation, however, when the whole society might die out, the weakest members of the group—the very old and the very young who impaired movement in the desperate search for food—might be abandoned or killed by community consent. But normally the stronger individuals would not try to save themselves at the expense of the group, and social reciprocity and more or less institutionalized "giveaways" of material possessions were normal events, not mere considerations of charity. Through hospitality and gift exchange, there was a constant give and take of ritual goods.

Prestige, status, and esteem in hunting and gathering societies were commonly gained through generosity and the holding of frequent giveaway rituals, which served as economic equalizers. For the headman, especially, a generous disposition tended to be a prerequisite for continuing influence. By giving to the members of his band he imposed upon them a kind of debt for as long as the gift was unrequited. Sahlins notes that in this sense the economic relationship between giver and receiver contributed to the political relationship between leader and follower. Among bands in many parts of the world, and tribes as well, generosity was expected not only from those who had some measure of authority, but also from any member of the group who had been fortunate in the hunt or had enjoyed some other windfall.

Were our Paleolithic ancestors inherently less selfish than we? More generous? More ethical? Not necessarily. Among hunters and gatherers the critical consideration was that each individual—including the best hunter, the headman, and the shaman—could not fail to recognize that his or her survival depended upon the welfare and survival of everyone else in the band. Exclusion from the group could be fatal. But there was a further consideration that favored generosity and material equality.

The most serious handicap of the hunting and gathering way of life was not low productivity of labor, but the drain upon local resources and consequent imminence of diminishing returns. As a result, hunters and gatherers did not hoard or stockpile material possessions. Indeed, it would have been dysfunctional for them to do so. As food supplies were depleted in any given locality, it was time for the band to move on. The lighter they traveled, the more food they were likely to acquire. Unnecessary possessions could be a serious impediment. Whatever temporary advantage might be achieved by the accumulation of material goods would be enjoyed at the expense of badly needed mobility. As Sahlins explains, "It would anchor the camp to an area soon to be depleted of natural food supplies."

In such relatively small, face-to-face, intensely participatory societies, there was often little or no need for penal sanctions as we conceive of them now. A wide range of crimes today emerges from concepts of private property and "legalized" inequalities in access to resources. A band might view an expanse of hunting and gathering territory as theirs, but

Migration by Barton Wright.

the concept of private property, insofar as it existed at all, was otherwise limited to clothing, weapons, and a few personal effects. Good behavior was to a large extent the outcome of social pressures from the group: early upbringing, expectations of relatives, immersion in lore and rituals, and the fear of criticism, scorn, or ostracism. In such small communities, a serious transgression tended to be a concern of everyone, and for the culprit there was no place to hide. Most members of a band were restrained from evil deeds by the high value attached to generosity and cooperative rather than competitive efforts, by the tremendous power of public opinion, and by their dependence upon other members of the group.

Our hunting and gathering forebears held animistic beliefs about the universe, the features of the earth and its plants and animals, and about themselves. These beliefs offered explanations for what our Stone Age ancestors did not understand in the world about them. Shamans, who often treated the sick and disabled, gave advice about dealing with nature and other problems of everyday life, and they were usually influential members of the group. In general Stone Age people did not assume the sharp dichotomy between people and animals or people and things that has been widespread in more recent times: human beings and the natural environment were perceived as elements of a single whole. People tried to negotiate or even collaborate with nature rather than fight it, intervene in massive ways, or otherwise seek to control it. Animistic beliefs, myths, and legends offered explanations for natural processes of the universe and shaped future expectations.

Tribal Government

As populations grew and new advances were made in technology, the band form of organization became inadequate. People developed new institutions to deal with each other and cope with the natural environment. If the size of a band exceeded 125 or 150 people, heavy strains were placed upon resources, and organizational arrangements that had been effective for smaller numbers of people were no longer adequate. At some threshold point, the society would have to split up, expand its territorial range, or develop a more efficient technology.

During the Neolithic or New Stone Age, the domestication of plants and animals made it possible for larger numbers of people to live in a limited territory. But more populous societies and new modes of living increased the potentials in the community for competition, conflict, and disintegration and thus required new decision and regulatory mechanisms to maintain stability. In many societies in various parts of the world the transition to a new level of organization was accomplished by the development of clans that cut across families and bands, thus tying them together into tribes.

The agricultural revolution of the Neolithic Age made it feasible for people to exploit the natural environment in new ways, and consequently the tribal level of organization achieved a greater cultural and institutional diversity than had been evident among bands. In his book *Primitive Social Organization,* anthropologist Elman Service describes how various tribal economies accomplished many different combinations of hunting, fishing, gathering, agriculture, and pastoralism which, combined with variations in habitat, encouraged a considerable range of social and political structures. Tribes normally ranged in size from a few hundred to perhaps 1,500 people. Depending upon climate, terrain, and related factors, each tribe might occupy between 5,000 and 15,000 square miles.

Whereas a band was a simple association of families, a tribe amounted to an association of kin groups which were themselves composed of bands. A tribe was likely to emerge as blood-related bands learned to maintain cohesion through clans, which cut across and tended to tie together two or more component groups. Where familial relations were thus extended and technological advances achieved, a more intensive exploitation of local resources was often possible, yielding a greater surplus. The first tribes may have developed in a few particularly favorable environments during the food-collecting Paleolithic Age. But it was the Neolithic revolution that brought the tribal form to dominance.

Tribal society remained essentially self-regulating, participatory, egalitarian, and lacking in political hierarchies and dominant groups. The major forces for integration were still kinship ties, common interests, and community activities; common religious beliefs and rituals; and the impulse toward collective action against outside attack. The necessities of life were freely shared, and decisions were made largely through face-to-face discussions and oratory. The headman of a tribe was usually referred to as a chief. He was normally a man of prestige and influence, but he did not have the political power or decision-making authority of a dictator, king, or modern president. However, as suggested by sociologist Robert MacIver in his book *The Modern State*, a chief's authority was likely to increase as the tribe grew in size and as divisions of labor became more complex with advances in agriculture and other technologies.

In a large tribe, many of the political functions were carried out by councilmen representing the people at large, rather than through daily face-to-face discussion and consensus seeking. Yet the tribe, as long as its membership did not greatly exceed the level of a thousand people, was small enough so that the whole body enjoyed the possibility of assembling on occasion, and virtually everyone had some knowledge of everyone else. Since neither the chief nor the council had institutionalized powers of coercion, tribal policy tended to be sensitive to the demands generated by the people. On the tribal level, as among the independent bands that preceded it, the concept of penal sanctions was virtually absent. Disputes were normally "talked out" by the parties and their respective relatives, and more serious transgressions were normally controlled by group pressures. According to anthropologist R.H. Lowie in *The Origin of the State*, a Blackfoot who had made a nuisance of himself would be held up to general ridicule amidst shrieks of laughter. The Crow and Hidatsa used "joking relatives," older kinsmen on the father's side of the family, to reprimand a tribesman who was not behaving properly. A culprit thus exposed and jeered at would, Lowie recounts, "feel like sinking into the ground with shame." Similarly, social anthropologist A.R. Radcliffe-Brown describes how members of African tribes used ridicule to correct the behavior of troublemakers.

Competition in various skills—hunting, dancing, foot racing, and the like—might be intense, but the rewards tended to be honorific. Competition for material goods was normally considered mean and miserly and was censured by the community. In many tribes a major criterion for leadership was the willingness to endure hardship and eschew material reward. Consciously or unconsciously, people knew from their own experience and from tribal folklore that the survival of the individual depended overwhelmingly upon the survival of the group.

Among some tribes (as well as bands) violence, both domestic and external, was rare. Others were characterized on occasion by internal violence such as murders or feuds but seldom engaged in warfare. Tribes in a third general category were warlike but had little domestic violence. Still other tribes were characterized by both internal and external violence. Almost universally, however, whatever warfare took place on band and tribal levels tended to be relatively underdeveloped, certainly as compared to the warfare engaged in at even the earliest state levels. Standing armies did not exist, and although there might be a war chief in addition to a civil chief, the concept of an institutionalized military hierarchy had not yet emerged.

The object of warfare was seldom to acquire new lands. Indians of the North American plains, for example, usually fought for revenge, to achieve glory, or, after the arrival of the white man, to acquire horses. Sometimes major tribal forces were pitted against each other, but this was rare. Among many tribes it was considered of the utmost importance that a war party return without losing a single man. To incur losses deliberately for strategic ends was often considered repulsive. From the deep interior of New Guinea anthropologists Robert Gardner and Karl Heider report how "warlike" Dani tribesmen engage in frequent and fearsome ritual battles characterized by imprecations and armed pantomime rather than by actual casualties, which seldom occur. (The attitude of the Dani toward warfare is illustrated by their willingness to call off a battle, in case of rain, to prevent their feathered headdresses from getting wet.)

The relatively large numbers of peaceful bands and tribes in many parts of the world may be explained in part by the vast expanses of territory contrasted to the small number of people, by the organizational characteristics of Paleolithic and Neolithic societies (the lack of coercive leadership and bureaucratic planning and supply structures), and by the limited range and killing power of available weapons. But there may have been other, less obvious influences. From studying the structures of large numbers of prestate societies, psychiatrist and research scholar Roderic Gorney has concluded that three conditions characterized those social orders that were conspicuously nonaggressive and nonviolent: 1) children were brought up to disperse their feelings of emotional attachment and dependency not only among parents and siblings but also among a wide array of grandparents, uncles, aunts, cousins, and other members of the community; 2) all members of such societies enjoyed relatively equal access to resources and benefits; and 3) each individual, by the same act and at the same time, clearly served both his or her own advantage and that of the group.

The Chiefdom: A Foreshadowing of the State

With population density increasing and hunting and gathering superceded by more advanced agriculture, the trend was away from egalitarianism and toward societies based on rank and much wider differentials in access to resources.

Again, observations should not lead us to conclude that our ancestors in prestate societies were necessarily less innately aggressive or bloodthirsty than those of us living in state-level societies. On the contrary, people in bands, tribes, and chiefdoms killed, tortured, and sometimes practiced cannibalism. But they lacked the domestic cohesion, the organizational skills, the resource surpluses, the transportation facilities, and the weapons to coerce or exploit each other systematically, to mount sustained military campaigns, or to capture, enslave, or kill large numbers of people. Organized warfare and conquest—like complexities in civil regulation—in most cases appear to be closely tied to relatively large populations, more advanced technology, complex social, political, economic, and military organization, and a capacity for accumulating surpluses in resources and human energy.

Tribal societies have normally encompassed from a few hundred to a few thousand people at most. For long periods of time, most of them have tended to remain relatively stable because they fitted the needs of their component bands. By producing more people to feed, clothe, and shelter, however, substantial increases in population invariably forced the tribe either to split into two or more independent groups or to devise new political, economic, and social institutions capable of providing for the enlarged community. In many widely separated parts of the world, the latter course led to the development of chiefdoms and often, but not always, the emergence of relatively systematic and large-scale agriculture as a prevailing technology. In some environments, advanced fishing and other techniques substituted for agriculture. Overall, however, in Egypt and Mesopotamia, India, China, and the Middle Americas, it was advanced agriculture that provided the economic substructure for change. Having developed new methods for growing and processing foods, our ancestors were able to store produce on a scale that had not been possible before and thus create surpluses. Thrift often emerged as an important value, and rights of private property began to be recognized. Depending on the type of agriculture practiced, families tended to settle on particular plots of land.

As some communities grew in population, they extended over two or more ecological zones where quite different technologies were appropriate: ocean fishing and agriculture, perhaps, or the cultivation of crops and cattle herding. New and more complex technologies encouraged more pronounced divisions of labor and exclusive specializations, which contributed, along with the need for exchange between different ecological zones, to alterations and new complexities in social and political organization. In response to such mixed environments, some communities developed intermediate forms—more complex than the typical tribe but not yet meeting the criteria of the state—which have been referred to as *chiefdoms*. Their emergence depended upon the accumulation of sharper and more complex divisions of labor, more technological specializations, more exchanges of materials between zones, and more accumulated surpluses than a tribal organization could successfully regulate. On this level, we discern the beginnings of institutions that eventually made possible the emergence of the state.

The development of chiefdoms in many parts of the world, including the Tigris-Euphrates Valley, the Indus and Yellow River basins, coastal Peru, and central Mexico, was associated with terraced land and the building of irrigation works. Compared with the archaic states and empires that developed subsequently in such areas, these earlier societies lacked the necessary capabilities for constructing huge interconnecting canals (which appeared later) and were thus unable to expand their activities and territorial boundaries beyond single-stream valleys. Despite these limitations, however, the practice of irrigation raised agriculture to new levels and provided a basis for new divisions of labor, new technical specializations, and new differentials in reward.

The chiefdom was largely familistic, kinship still providing powerful ties, but not egalitarian. There was no private property in resources or entrepreneurial market commerce, yet there was unequal control over raw materials, production, and the distribution of goods. Although the chiefdom had no government in the more structured and institutionalized sense, it did have rank hierarchies and centralized authority.

Chiefdoms of the Northwest Pacific coast, as well as in other parts of the world, often kept a few slaves and observed differences in rank from the chief to the lowest commoner, but there were no clear-cut economic or social classes. Anthropologist Philip Drucker suggests that, according to the nearness or distance in his relationship to the chief, each individual was in a class by himself. As in chiefdoms elsewhere, wealth was an extremely important factor in determining rank among Indians of Northwest Pacific coast chiefdoms.

A chiefdom, unlike a tribe, yielded to its chief the ability to plan, organize, and deploy public labor—but without the institutionalized political power that kings of even the most archaic states employed. The chiefship was a recognized "office," and an important aspect of it was the incumbent's ability to apportion labor for terracing and irrigation. With relatively centralized control of the distribution of goods, the chief could support a range of specialized workers. The chief's weakness came from his lack of a legalized monopoly of violence for enforcement of his will. As in bands and tribes, his control over the lives and property of his people depended upon the prestige of his position and the force of his own personality, but wealth gave him additional power.

As a redistributional economy, according to anthropologist Peter Farb in his book *Man's Rise To Civilization as Shown by the Indians of North America*, a chiefdom had possibilities for territorial expansion which earlier forms of society had lacked. Neither bands nor tribes had been able to acquire the economic surpluses or to develop the complex institutions required for integrating conquered peoples into their societies and maintaining an extended territorial base. Chiefdoms, on the other hand, easily assimilated conquered peoples and occupied their lands, and that, Farb states, "is why true warfare appears for the first time at this level of social organization."

Thomas Hobbes believed that during the time when human beings existed without a common power "to keep them all in awe," they necessarily lived in a condition of war in which everyone was pitted against everyone else. In such condition there was no place for society, culture, or industry. People lived in continual fear and danger of violent death. But from today's perspective it appears that almost the opposite may be true: the overall trend through human prehistory and history may have been toward greater domestic and external violence rather than less.

In fact, the potential for violence in prestate societies appears to have been severely limited. Examples of societies that have been most truly peaceful—both externally and in their domestic affairs—have normally been drawn from among bands, tribes, or even chiefdoms, but seldom from states or empires. And even among prestate peoples who have been described as warlike, the numbers of casualties and amount of material destruction have usually been comparatively limited. Including preparations and post-battle ceremonials, the amount of time and attention devoted to actual hostilities also tended to be small. Sustained military programs, highly organized campaigns, and the massive slaughtering of civilians as well as soldiers are relatively modern phenomena—the inventions of larger societies, more advanced technologies, and more complex orders of organization and government.

This discussion of our early forebears reveals that people's values and relationships are not constant, but vary with substantial changes in population and advances in technology. The trend from band to tribe to chiefdom involved changes in human values as well as organizational changes. Population increases and more advanced technologies yielded larger societies, which required new social, economic, and political institutions in order to provide stability and to meet people's demands. These changes created more centralized control and the crude beginnings of bureaucracy. Equal access to resources, political and economic decision making, and many social benefits decreased as more and more wealth accumulated at the top. The trend was only beginning, however. The next chapter will indicate some of the ways in which human societies were transformed with the emergence of the state.

Scenes of rural life, from grave of Ti at Saqqara.

CHAPTER THREE

THE EMERGENCE OF THE STATE

DATING FROM ABOUT 5000 B.C., rising populations, more sophisticated technologies, agricultural surpluses, and new distribution and storage systems made craft and class specializations both possible and necessary. These agricultural surpluses not only supported larger numbers of people, but also provided opportunities for planning, experimentation, and innovation that were not possible on a hand-to-mouth level of existence. The advancement of agricultural techniques prepared the way for the first archaic states. Once a society had begun to grow and store grain, for example, it was possible not only to prepare for famine years but also to feed concentrations of slave or corvée labor and to provision an extended military campaign. These surpluses provided new possibilities, too, for the manipulation of resources in competitions for wealth, power, domination, status, or prestige. By making it feasible to use resources, as well as ranks and statuses, for rewarding "success," chiefdoms established a base for dividing people into classes.

Despite the superior capacity of chiefdoms, as compared with bands and tribes, for serving larger numbers of people, overseeing diverse ecological zones, and generating surpluses, they were severely limited in their potential. Their organizational arrangements were inadequate for imposing the discipline that was necessary for acquiring, processing, and systematically distributing resources among increasingly large numbers of people. In many parts of the world, therefore, chiefdoms—

under intensified population pressures—gave way to archaic states as new agricultural and other techniques were developed.

In earlier chapters we have contested the idea that "human nature" is uniform, constant, or static. This chapter develops the thesis that with the emergence of the state major changes took place in human values, attitudes, dispositions, and behaviors. The chapter also lays a groundwork for the further proposition that many contemporary trends in human affairs—including a number that seem troublesome, threatening, even potentially catastrophic—are legacies of the state level of human development rather than the result of factors inherent in human nature per se.

Explanations for the emergence of the state tend to fall into two main categories, the voluntaristic and the coercive. If we accept the first view, we may conclude that tribes or chiefdoms combined more or less spontaneously into states much as bands combined into tribes during earlier stages of sociocultural evolution. We may postulate, for example, that the people voluntarily extended to their chief, now their king, the right and power of domestic coercion in order to strengthen the society, increase its cohesion, and enhance its ability to protect itself from outside enemies.

As indicated in the preceding chapter, chiefdoms in various parts of the world had built impressive irrigation systems well before the emergence of state levels of organization, but often they were limited by terrain or other obstacles to a single river valley. When such limitations were eventually overcome, the logic of the situation led to the construction of huge interconnecting canals. Once a project of this magnitude was well under way, Elman Service notes in *Primitive Social Organization*, "the societies were transformed to a new level." In Mexico, Egypt, Mesopotamia, China, and elsewhere, the development of such waterworks made large-scale agriculture possible in arid and semiarid environments. In order to build them, however, it was necessary to organize large numbers of people into gangs of corvée labor under the direction of corps of overseers. Construction of complex irrigation works also required administrative arrangements for supplying the workers. And specialists were needed to survey the land, measure water volume, keep track of time, and predict the weather. The development of these technologies contributed in important ways to the emergence of ancient states and the early civilizations that they represented.

While incorporating similar observations about the organizational functions and complexities of the early state, coercion theories, by contrast, postulate that people initially fell subject to state authority through some threat or application of force—possibly outright conquest. If we accept this perspective, we can visualize certain tribes or chiefdoms—perhaps those whose growing populations and advancing technologies enhanced both their capabilities and their demands for food and other resources—conquering, absorbing, controlling, and in many cases enslaving weaker societies around their peripheries. By exploiting the subdued populations economically, the victors were then able to sustain themselves as a ruling class more or less indefinitely. According to anthropologist Robert Carneiro in "A Theory of the Origin of the State" (*Science*, August 21, 1970), wars between societies thus created the coercive governmental structures that are characteristic of societies on the state level, and also brought about many political, economic, and military institutions that greatly increased the efficiency of corporate action against neighboring societies.

It is possible, of course, that some primitive states emerged voluntaristically and others as a result of threat of coercion or actual conquest.

A Legal Monopoly of Force

A true state, however underdeveloped or democratic, can be distinguished from a band, tribe, or chiefdom, according to Service, by the presence of "the consistent threat of force by a body of persons legitimately constituted to use it." In whatever way a given elite achieves power and justifies its right to rule, this monopoly of force serves as an instrument for maintaining domestic law and order, for defending the state from enemies, and for protecting its external interests. This institutionalized and potentially powerful decision and control apparatus, which claims to oversee and override all other organizations within its boundaries, may be displayed in a variety of forms by quite disparate societies with populations ranging anywhere from a few thousand to many millions. In addition to standing armies and specialized police forces of some kind, states have also developed multitiered and often quite complex bureaucratic hierarchies, elaborate systems of taxation, and unprecedented possibilities for the accumulation of private and/or public surpluses, treasure, or capital. In such respects the differences between ancient and modern states are largely of detail and degree rather than of function or kind.

Some scholars believe that the emergence of the earliest states—in China, India, Mesopotamia, Egypt, Mexico, Peru, and elsewhere—depended upon large-scale, highly institutionalized slavery. Without such massive sources of compulsory labor, the reasoning goes, a society could not accumulate the concentration of surplus capital that was necessary for even the most primitive state to develop. Certainly the construction

Queen Nefertari to the side of one of the tomb statues of King Ramses II, at Luxor.

of huge pyramids, public buildings, and water systems that characterized many of the most ancient states required some form of cheap, highly organized mass labor.

At the heart of the development of the state was the task of maintaining general social order. And essential to the maintenance of the general social order is the need to defend the stratification of the society, the different categories of population based on divisions of labor and access to basic resources. To a large extent it is the institutions and agencies of a state—some formal, others informal—that maintain the stratification and general social order. A major change in the structure of a society normally depends upon alterations in the institutions and agencies.

State structures are both the outcome and the regulators of competition between sectors of the society. It is not uncommon for the religion of the society to rationalize or justify the structure and values of the state, although there have also been instances where the state and religious hierarchies were at odds. Often the prevailing religion developed hierarchical structures paralleling those of the state. In some societies the high priests advised the king. In others, the monarch served also as the high priest. Nearly all these essentially state-level phenomena—like the state itself—are comparatively recent social inventions compared with band and tribal forms.

In most state-level societies, those who possess resources (through legal ownership) and those who control the flow and distribution of resources (quite apart from what they may or may not "own" in a strictly legal sense) tend to enjoy preferential access to other benefits—social status, prestige, access for themselves and members of their families to education, travel, cultural advantages, and the like.

As classes and privileged ranks emerged, so did the values required to rationalize and even justify the differences. Some values might be shared widely by all sectors of a society. In terms of family obligations, loyalties, inheritance procedures, and so forth, there might be many parallels from one class stratum to another. But the larger, more encompassing value system, the *collective conscience*, maintained sharp distinctions between the levels and made explicit how the societal benefits and costs were to be distributed. Thus, unlike the band or tribe where value differences were largely associated with age or sex, societies on the state level applied alternate sets of values according to economic or social class and enforced them, when necessary, by armed might. In these terms, the political and economic hierarchies of a society—the gross but "legal" inequities in class, wealth, and political or military power—were legitimized by the value hierarchy. An important function of state legal systems was to recognize, codify, and defend the rights, privileges, and obligations of the various hierarchies and class structures which the society had produced.

Warfare and, indeed, all kinds of legitimized violent coercion and killing became monopolies of the state and were thereafter carried out quite consciously and legally in defense of state interests and institutions but only at times, in places, and under the specific conditions determined by the ruling elite. At the band or tribal levels a headman or chief could not muster a war party unless he was supported by a wide consensus. If any considerable number of those of fighting age were not predisposed toward hostilities, they had to be won over by oratory, shaming, promise of booty, or other inducement. Within a chiefdom, the chief was more powerful than anyone else in his society and he could lead other men into battle, but like his counterparts on the band and tribal levels, he lacked the exclusive right to use force. This was a severe limitation compared to the position of a king or emperor. Whatever violence the chief might employ was not the only legitimized force that existed in the society. Families or clans might feud with one another; a band of warriors might set out independently to raid a neighboring chiefdom; a clan might inflict punishment on some offender.

In a state, by contrast, no one can use force legally except the state itself—more specifically, the ruler and his legally sanctioned agents such as the police and the army. Within a state structure, as noted by Service, feuding is viewed as an unspeakable crime and is punished severely, since its very existence means that someone aside from the state itself is exercising force. A king, unlike any leader on the band, tribe, or chiefdom levels, could thus rely on the civil or military power of his office to impose and enforce a levy or draw on his treasury to hire mercenaries.

Even today among states that consider themselves democratic, the police are called out in force whenever fundamental institutions are challenged, and if civil police power is not sufficient, the militia, reserves, or regular forces may be called upon to lend assistance. Such considerations are so commonplace that we almost take them for granted, noting only the more spectacular or tragic deviations from the norm of any given society. Yet against the background of up to four million years of human existence, these wide differentials in access to resources and benefits are a newly emergent phenomenon, dating largely from the appearance of the state. And the state, in turn, even in its most primitive form, could not have developed without increases in population, advances in technology, and the growth of economic surpluses well beyond what bands, tribes, and chiefdoms had been able to achieve.

Differences in rank, status, power, influence, and access to resources and benefits create the potential for competition among individuals and among whole sectors of a society even though the various people involved may be unable—or, for various reasons, may be unwilling—to compete. Unless they can join forces in some organized way, the very poor or weak are incapable of challenging the very rich or powerful. Both the law and armed might are usually ranged against them. Moreover, to the extent that the overarching values of the society have been widely internalized by the populace, the exploited classes are often not disposed to question the rationale or justice of their deprivations. In this way, the differential capabilities, the differential accesses to resources and benefits, the inherent competitions, and the consequent hierarchies (political, economic, and social) may become mirrored in the consciousness of large numbers of people in a society to such an extent that major changes in these arrangements and relationships are difficult to achieve.

Intensified Competition: A New Driving Force

It is a central thesis of this book that class and bureaucratic hierarchies emerged as the result of enhanced competition among growing populations possessing more advanced technologies. But such hierarchies had effects of their own—disciplining economic and political enterprises, making further technological advances possible, and, at the same time, exacerbating competition for resources among individuals, classes, and whole societies. Over long periods of time the persistent expansion of competitive institutions and hierarchical frameworks in many societies has resulted in the widespread acceptance of intense competition as a desirable and even inherent human value. Often this acceptance is found among people in lower hierarchies or classes, who consistently stand to lose rather than gain by continuing competition for resources, status, prestige, and power.

Competition refers to rivalry between two or more individuals or groups for some prize. The prize may involve either a constant or expanding surplus within a society; a valuable but diminishing resource; a rank, status, or position of power within a society; or some other social, economic, political, or cultural advantage. Competition may also be viewed as an effort on the part of each individual or group to keep ahead of the rival in some type of race, even just "keeping ahead of the Joneses" in day-to-day life. As Anatol Rapoport notes in *Fights, Games, and Debates*, "the efficient are rewarded and the inefficient eliminated," or at least penalized in the currency of whatever game is being played. The prize may be fixed: a particular resource; an absolute level of industrial, military, or other capability; a constant rate of growth; a particular office; or a wage or salary level. Or, the prize may be relative and subject to change: achieving or maintaining "first place" in terms of production, armament, wealth, power, prestige. There is a critical difference between competitions that involve vital resources, wealth, influence, or power and those—such as competing for a poetry prize—that do not. In this book we are concerned primarily with the former category, those competitions that elevate a relatively small number of people into positions of economic or political power and leave others at serious disadvantage.

From one perspective, economic competition is not a goal in the sense that social, political, and military competition tend to be. An important economic function of competition is to discipline the various participants in a society to provide their goods and services skillfully, efficiently, and cheaply. In line with this specialized perspective, the concept of "perfect competition" in the field of economics requires that the largest firm in an industry, for example, make no more than a small fraction of the total sales or purchases of all the firms in that industry. The concept therefore implies that there will be many separate firms within a single industry and that they will act independently, without conspiratorial price fixing or other collusion. Perfect competition further requires that all the participants in a particular market have perfect knowledge to buy and sell—that none is ignorant of the production and pricing policies of any other. From the actual perspective of a day-to-day participant in the "economic game," however, the role of economic competition may look quite different. A small competitor may perceive himself at a severe disadvantage compared to a large firm (perhaps a monopoly) in terms of obtaining capital, raw materials, and technology; securing markets; or setting prices. So, too, from the perspective of a whole society, economic competition may involve social or political side effects that were not anticipated or provided for. Specifically, it may involve the stakes that help determine a country's relative power or the welfare, status, influence, and perhaps even the survival of an individual within the particular society.

Many competitions arise from what parties *think* may happen—from their anxieties, prejudices, fears, and uncertainties—rather than from any phenomenon that is actually threatening. Conversely, even when parties are aware of a potential for competition, they may refrain from it. It is also possible, especially within a large society or an organization of considerable size, for people to be in competition without being aware of it.

Competition may, and frequently does, become transformed into conflict and even violence. Whether or not this transformation occurs may depend upon whether the parties see themselves as basically incompatible and whether they consider the issues involved—the outcome or the prize—important.

Many different types of states have developed in various parts of the world during recent millennia, and at first glance they may not seem to have much in common—especially as between an archaic state in ancient Mesopotamia, Egypt, or Mexico and the United States or the Soviet Union today. Most scholars agree with biologist Ludwig von Bertalanffy, however, that the evolution of human societies often proceeds along multiple paths, in different sequences, and with great variations in degrees of absolutism, pluralism, democracy, and other important details. Nearly all types of states have involved competition for critical resources and for the social and political rewards that accompany such access. This fundamental tendency toward competition, in turn, has had a powerful influence upon a wide variety of institutions on the state level of organization.

Competition of one type or another contributes to the development of hierarchies of rank, status, class, power, influence, and access to resources and benefits—and the value hierarchies to rationalize and justify them—which have characterized the state since it first emerged as a system of governance. Indeed, these phenomena and the processes that produce them virtually define the state. But the forms and details of these hierarchies have differed considerably from culture to culture. The institutional structures of Athens were quite different from those of Egypt or Persia, even though some of the functions were similar. Usually the characteristics of such hierarchies have varied with the nature of the competition, which has reflected, in turn, the requirements of the society for making a living in its particular environment. Thus, agricultural societies have tended to develop characteristic institutions according to whether they depended upon rainfall farming or vast irrigation projects such as those which characterized the archaic land-based empires of China, India, Mesopotamia, Egypt, Mexico, and Peru. And from far back in history we find commercially based city-states—whether among the Phoenicians, the ancient Greeks, or late medieval and early Renaissance Italians—developing political forms appropriate for tradesmen and the specialized requirements of buying, selling, and shipping. In many instances, from Phoenicia to Britain after the sixteenth century, commercial states expanded into far-flung sea-lane, as contrasted to land-based, empires.

Agricultural states often experienced bitter competition between elite families of landholding warriors who struggled for further territories or for the throne itself. Other levels of such societies were normally

Three boats from the flotilla of the Vizier Meket Re.

characterized by deep-rooted, relatively inflexible competition wherein members of the landholding, warlord elites kept the masses in serfdom or slavery for generation upon generation. In societies based upon rainfall farming, various land-tenure and other feudal arrangements frequently tied the serfs and even the relatively free tenants to plots of soil, where custom and the day-to-day drudge for survival kept them at the mercy of their exploiters.

So, too, in societies based upon large-scale irrigation, the discipline of corvée labor constrained the slave or serf from overt competition—even though, overall, the hierarchy of advantage from the laborers to the nobles, the high priests, and the monarch himself was ruthlessly competitive in its implications. Often the easiest way to rise in the hierarchy was to associate oneself with an ambitious warlord or to organize an armed force of one's own. Seldom in intervals of a hundred years or more were conditions in a society right for the slaves, serfs, or other oppressed masses to rebel, and, even then, such rebellions often failed.

Commercial states opened the door for a wholly new concept of competition based initially upon shrewd barter and subsequently upon the leverages created by such mechanisms as coinage, investment, credit, interest, and the like. Within such societies the poorest clerk, handyman, peasant, or runaway slave occasionally became rich. By the latter part of the Middle Ages these developments had created unprecedented opportunities, seized upon again and again in Florence, Pisa, Venice, and other Italian cities, whereby runaway peasants hired out to independent entrepreneurs and eventually, by skillful playing of the competitive game, rose to become merchants, bankers, and political oligarchs. According to historian Ferdinand Schevill in his book *Medieval and Renaissance Florence*, in Italy as early as the thirteenth century many great rural barons of the Tuscan countryside thus "had to suffer the gradual transfer of their houses and lands to the Spini, the Mozzi, the Frescobaldi, the Peruzzi, and other similar urban residents," who had risen "from a level akin to that of small pawnshop dealers to the status of great bankers and, forgetting their plebeian origin, looked upon themselves in comparison with their fellow-townsmen as born to the purple." Centuries later, the potential for this type of competition was vastly enhanced by the fourth great system break, the industrial revolution, marked by the harnessing of steam as a new source of energy and giving rise to whole generations of new elites.

Some Domestic Consequences of Growth

In growing societies, competitive striving and expected personal advancement tended to be encouraged—especially among more aggressive individuals and groups—and to replace, over time, the egalitarianism of hunting and gathering peoples. With the emergence of the state, ever more complex divisions of labor have contributed to growth in various dimensions, to the development of classes, and to strong possibilities of conflict between different layers of society. (By growth we refer first of all to increases in population and advances in technology. But increases in capital surplus, enhanced productivity, and the ability to acquire, transform, and apply larger amounts of energy and other resources are also manifestations of growth.) Wherever growth takes place, it is likely to contribute to competition and scarcity in complex ways. Increases in population and advances in technology not only generate greater demands for resources, they may also result in pollution of the environment, depletion of more readily available resources, and the reaching out for new resources farther and farther from home territory.

As their capabilities increased, human beings began to perceive themselves as masters over nature, and it seemed to follow that the earth and all the other creatures must have been created for their purposes. Prior to the flood, according to the Old Testament, God enjoined all creatures to be fruitful and multiply, but human beings were specifically commanded to take possession of the earth. After the flood, God issued similar injunctions to Noah and his sons. Classical writers of the West, especially after Heraclitus, developed the idea further: "We are the absolute masters of what the earth produces," wrote Cicero. "By our hands we endeavor . . . to make, as it were, another Nature."

Human beings have always possessed means of altering and to some extent damaging the natural environment. Especially with control of fire, people had the possibility of burning large tracts of forest and grasslands. During most of the Paleolithic and early Neolithic Ages, however, the limited number of people and the simplicity of their tools and weapons kept to a minimum the damage that could be done. But the great agricultural revolution of the Neolithic Age, along with the emergence of the state with its centralized authority and capacity for organizing labor and marshaling resources, brought about major changes.

Plato, the Chinese philosopher Mencius, Strabo in his *Geography*, and many other classical writers recorded how intensive grazing, overcultivation, the cutting of timber, and other human undertakings polluted local environments and depleted vital resources in many parts of the ancient world. Thus, extensive areas in Europe, Asia, Africa, Mexico, Peru, and elsewhere suffered severe depredation well before the industrial revolution. Since then, the consequences of increasing populations and advancing technologies have spread from such relatively local areas of human concentration to the land, sea, and air around much of the globe.

Some scholars believe that the great agricultural revolution of the late Neolithic Age brought about the deepest single transformation in human nature—at least subsequent to man's control over fire. According to this view the discipline of sophisticated agriculture made whole populations sedentary, territorial, ambitious, acquisitive, thrifty, capable of extended foresight and planning, self-consciously competitive, and willing to deny themselves short-term advantages in order to reap greater gains later on.

Other scholars, while recognizing the importance of the discipline imposed upon people by relatively advanced agriculture, are more concerned with the further changes in human attitudes and behavior that took place with the development of commerce and sophisticated methods of finance. Advances in commerce and concentrations of capital produced characteristic economic and political processes which were different from those in societies that were predominantly agricultural. In states where commerce was the prevailing technology, certain assumptions, relationships, and processes of the marketplace tended to be reflected in the political structure. Buying and selling, for example, assume a certain rough equality among the parties. One party may be richer than the other or more skillful in the bargaining process, but normally they carry out their negotiations on the assumption that each is a free agent who is in a position to buy, sell, make contracts, take responsibility for indebtedness, and so forth. Such relationships are quite different from those between master and slave, serf and landowner, warrior and warlord, or noble and monarch (although many such institutions characterizing agriculturally based societies often survived in essentially commercial and in "mixed" societies as well).

In a crude way, the various economic relationships and interactions among free merchants were often paralleled by appropriate political institutions and processes. Thus economic and political structures both assumed a free and legally equal citizenry, the negotiation of political as well as commercial issues, and bargaining over issues as well as goods. It was logical that an economy depending upon commercial contracts would be associated with a government legitimatized by political contract or the like—institutions and procedures that were developed among the Athenians, Phoenicians, Carthaginians, and later the citizens of Italian city-states of the late Middle Ages. As with buying, selling, and other commercial processes, moreover, the assumptions of freedom, independence, and legal equality did not constrain the more efficient and effective citizens from maximizing their rewards—political power and influence as well as economic affluence—even at the expense of the less efficient and effective.

Nor did these innovations in the economic and political structures of the commercial state reduce the levels of hierarchy, as compared with those in agricultural states. Indeed, over the long run, and down to the present, the trend has been toward greater and greater increases in hierarchy. Not only did commercial states maintain slaves in many instances as well as extensive working classes, they also gave rise to various gradations among the merchants themselves and created special niches for lawyers, scholars, medical men, and other specialists. Institutionalized slavery has now virtually disappeared, but hierarchical levels and wide differences among people in terms of social, political, and economic power and general access to resources and benefits have tended to become accepted more or less as a matter of course.

To a considerable extent the legal systems of states have been founded upon assumptions of economic, if not political, inequality, and oftentimes even substantial numbers of those who lose by such gradations so internalize class and income distinctions that they are quite prepared to accept and even defend them. On the other hand, to the extent that considerable numbers of the less efficient, less effective members of a society have internalized the values of growth, aggressive competition, and advancement—and especially if for some reason their rewards fall significantly short of their expectations—they may raise their demands and take actions, sometimes in the form of armed rebellions, that seriously threaten the privileges and other rewards of the elite groups. The outcome of such rebellions has often depended not only upon the amount of force the state could muster in order to put down the disorder but also upon its general capacity for functioning socially, economically, and politically. The solution in many societies has been to increase production and wealth by further stimulating national growth of one kind or another, thus providing at least some people at the lower levels with increases in income and their general standard of living without substantially reducing the relative share of the elite. Overall, such activities often have had the effect of further increasing the demands for resources.

A great many human benefits have resulted from technological advancement, economic growth, and the development of political institutions at the state level. Indeed, we have become so accustomed to the fruits of human progress that we can scarcely imagine life without them. This is true whether we refer to rapid transportation and communications facilities, modern medicine and public health, labor-saving devices and the proliferation of material conveniences and luxuries that are increasingly available even to the relatively disadvantaged—or to a wide array of economic and political arrangements that we tend to take for granted. Seemingly, in the whole course of our three million years or so as a species, human beings have "never had it so good." Yet, it is becoming more and more evident that many of these benefits also contribute to a host of troubles ranging from pollution of the land, water, and air to urban crowding, suburban sprawl, clogged freeways, uncontrollable bureaucracies, taxation, inflation, unemployment, and so on. Does this mean that every benefit exacts a balancing cost? That progress in one dimension is likely to involve retrogression in another?

External Expansion as an Outcome of Domestic Growth

So far in this chapter we have focused upon competition within a society itself. But just as increasing populations, combined with emergent technologies, created new possibilities for domestic competitions, so, too, these overall growth trends brought about changes in competition between societies.

A large part of the activities undertaken by a society in order to meet both public and private demands are carried on inside its own territorial limits—from its farmlands, forests, mines, lakes, rivers, and so forth. A society is likely to turn outward, however, to the extent that demands cannot be met by domestically available resources or to the extent that such resources can be acquired more economically outside territorial limits (either directly or through exchange in foreign markets) or to the extent that in one way or another a more favorable return on investment of effort or resources can be achieved by so doing. A society may reach outward in order to conserve its own domestic resources. Some extended efforts may take the form of exploration, discovery, conquest, emigration, commerce, investment, or other activities.

As societies grow, their activities expand and their demands increase. Hunting and gathering bands or tribes, as well as pastoral nomads, normally moved into new space when their immediate environment became seriously polluted or devoid of resources. Permanent agricultural settlements and territorially based states, on the other hand, have had to obtain outside resources by trade, expanding into adjacent territory, establishing overseas colonies, and so forth. As such societies reach out in search of additional resources to satisfy their demands, their activities tend to overlap the activities of other societies, thus generating competition. In the long run, increasing demands and competitions contribute to scarcities of resources. Ancient Rome, sixteenth-century Spain, seventeenth-century Britain and France, the United States during the nineteenth century, and Russia during the eighteenth, nineteenth, and well into the twentieth century experienced territorial expansion that correlated highly with population and technological growth.

Sumerian mosaic, *The Standard of Ur*.

Whether a people obtain the resources that are in demand locally or from foreign sources, they must have developed whatever specialized capabilities are needed in order to get and use the materials they seek. By specialized capabilities, we refer to specific applications of technology that are required to obtain a particular material or to process it for a desired outcome. Agriculture, commerce, transportation, communication, military and naval activities, education, health, welfare, and so forth require the development of specialized capabilities of one kind or another. This disposition to expand tends to be generated by increases in the home population combined with technological and economic development within the high-capability society.

Societies have often undertaken activities beyond their borders that were distinct from the acquisition of resources. They have explored distant lands for the sake of scientific investigation, missionaries have gone out to win religious converts, and tourists have traveled for pleasure and relaxation. A society might also reach out for markets rather than for resources.

Toward the close of the Middle Ages new technologies in Europe, many of them borrowed from the Arabs, brought about important changes in the organization and techniques of commerce, finance, shipbuilding, and navigation. These developments led, in turn, to unprecedented explorations of the globe by Italians, Portuguese, Spanish, French, Dutch, and other European peoples who penetrated more and more of the Americas, Asia, and Africa, and brought back a wide range of materials (many of them new to Europe) as well as enormous quantities of precious metals. This expansion of activity built huge surpluses in a number of European countries and, in some, laid financial foundations for the subsequent industrial development. In the course of this commercial growth and expansion, the new nation-states of Europe, whose initial development had often proceeded from an agricultural base, increasingly invoked values and produced political institutions reminiscent of those characterizing ancient city-states in Greece and elsewhere that depended heavily on commerce. Generally, those European states that did not develop such forms and values (Spain and Portugal, for example) failed also to move from exploration and the accumulation of treasure to large-scale investment in commerce, finance, and industry.

With the industrial revolution, the technology of commerce combined with the technology of the new machines to bring about major transformations within the industrialized states, in relationships between such states, and in relationships between them and other parts of the world where industrialization had not yet taken place. Among the changes that took place were huge accumulations of capital, the harnessing of vast amounts of mechanical energy, and rising standards of living and consumption. As people became accustomed to greater affluence, their expectations rose to encompass further conveniences and luxuries of life, with the result that they made even greater demands upon the economy, the government, and the society-at-large.

Accompanying these changes were important alterations in the world views and the values of people at different levels of society. Machines became important elements in daily life and altered human beliefs, preferences, and aspirations in a great many different ways. Competition for jobs, money, advancement, political influence, and social status became acute in many parts of an industrializing society. Demands arose for greater amounts and varieties of resources, many of them originating in parts of the world that were far removed from the centers of rapid technological development.

The tendency of a society to extend its activities beyond home territory often contributes to the conquest and sometimes to the exploitation of lower-capability societies occupying the territories that have been incorporated—as well as to conflicts with other states with interests in the same region. Thus, in expanding across the Appalachians, the Great Plains, and on to the West Coast, Americans conquered or enveloped Indian bands, tribes, and chiefdoms representing Stone Age levels of development. And in the Southwest we fought a war with Mexico, which seemed to block our way, and thus obtained vast new territories extending from Texas and Colorado to California. The prevailing values of an expanding society have frequently included elaborate justification for the conquest and domination of "uncivilized," "primitive," or "underdeveloped" peoples.

To the extent that they undertake activities beyond the boundaries of their own society, individuals, groups, commercial firms, and governmental agencies are likely to develop interests in newly explored territories or in other countries. These activities and interests can be economic, scientific, religious, educational, political, strategic, and so forth. Such an undertaking becomes a national interest when the country of origin is disposed to support or defend it economically, diplomatically, militarily, or by other means. Commercial, military, or tourist activities have become clearly identifiable national interests, for example, at whatever point the home country is prepared to issue a protest, establish an embargo, dispatch a gunboat, or land marines in their behalf. Any of these activities can affect a country's relations with other countries. Commercial, financial, military, and naval activities are likely to be especially significant, as is the acquisition of colonial territory or direct interference by a stronger country into the politics and economics of a weaker country.

High-capability societies, in expanding their activities and interests, frequently not only dominate or conquer weaker peoples, but also develop the feeling that interests thus established ought to be defended from encroachment by other countries. The desire to achieve and maintain law and order (as defined by the national leadership) and protect national interests (or large private interests) in far-off places may lead to the establishment of protectorates or other devices to control petty principalities or weaker states, or to the equipping and partial financing of client chiefs, warlords, or other rulers who can be induced to oppose rivals of the expanding state.

To the extent that two (or more) countries with high capabilities and expanding interests extend their activities and psychopolitical borders outward, there is a strong probability that sooner or later the two opposing perimeters of interest will intersect. Often the leaders of an aspiring but still somewhat weaker or less prestigious power feel that their country is being encircled by its rivals. Imperial Germany prior to World War I, Nazi Germany before World War II, and Japan during the years immediately prior to the attack on Pearl Harbor all complained of being encircled. When this happens, we may expect the competition to intensify and tend to become transformed into conflict and perhaps a cold war or arms race. In such circumstances, writes political scientist J. David Singer in *The Nature of Human Conflict* (E.B. McNeil, ed.), "One nation's security must inevitably be—in an environment of relative anarchy—another nation's insecurity." The two powers are likely to see themselves as competitors for influence and control on the high seas or in some land region, such as Southeast Asia or the Middle East, that is resource rich or is perceived as a key to strategic advantage.

International politics is in considerable part a competition for power. By power we mean a country's ability to act, to influence or control other countries, and to evade, resist, or deter the authority of other countries. Power may refer as much to what a country can do, or is thought to be able to do, as it does to what the country actually does or has done. Power may involve a country's ability to increase its ranges of opportunity and choice; to secure and maintain sea lanes, overland trade routes, and other means of access to resources or markets; to pursue technological or economic growth; to gain or protect a position of status or prestige; to achieve a strategic advantage; and so forth. The concept of power implies inequality.

In seeking, for whatever reasons, to strengthen its own position, each country is likely to validate the competitive anxieties of its rival. The primary demand for resources or markets in each competing country is likely to be generated by domestic growth processes, but as resources are depleted or markets flooded, competition between rivals is likely to exacerbate the demand and thus add to the contest.

Competition, especially for scarce resources (including prestige, influence, or power or the more tangible resources perceived as contributing to prestige, influence, or power), may give rise to "antagonizing," which psychologist Arthur Gladstone has defined as "the process by which each side forms an increasingly unfavorable picture of the other as evil, hostile, and dangerous." No matter which side starts it, the process tends to become mutual. "When one side criticizes, distrusts, ridicules, or denounces the other, the other side is likely to reply in kind." The more intense the competition, the greater is the probability of a change in the character of the interactions "from insult to injury." Thus, Gladstone continues, competition often leads "to nonviolent conflict, which leads in turn to an arms race which may then lead to crisis, which increases the probabilities of war."

The arms race constitutes an especially virulent type of competition in which the defense establishments of rival countries get interlocked into a rising spiral. Such external contributions to an arms race may be exacerbated by domestic influences. The development and manufacture of armaments can provide enticing benefits for a great many people, not only defense bureaucrats, high military officers, and the tsars of weapons-making, but also inventors, engineers, construction firms, clerks, foremen, craftsmen, warehousemen, and even whole communities where large numbers of people are employed in making arms or building ships, aircraft, or missiles. But often it is easier to obtain public funds for new weapons by minimizing these considerations and focusing upon an outside threat—whether real, imagined, or fabricated. Thus, the two processes, the domestic and the external, may reinforce each other in many situations.

There are analogies and connections between the arms race—the competition for supremacy in weaponry—and competitions for resources (especially as they become scarce), rank, status, power, influence, strategic advantage, and even control of information (itself a potential source of power). In fact, the struggle for critical resources, a variety of complex economic competitions, arms races, and the like may be viewed as mechanisms that sort countries out and distribute them in international hierarchies according to their broad capabilities.

The Cybernetic Revolution: Today's System Break

If we envisage the long, scarcely rising slope that characterizes human population growth, technological advancement, and organizational sophistication over the better part of man's existence as a species, we can infer that a member of a Paleolithic band, a Neolithic tribe, or even an archaic state did not witness much fundamental change in the course of his or her lifetime. This is no longer true today. Both population growth and technological advances are now so rapid in many societies that social knowledge can scarcely keep pace.

Especially since the beginning of the industrial revolution, growth and competition have affected—even transformed—both societies and individual human beings in virtually all parts of the world. Indeed, to a considerable extent the long tenure and relative stability of the state as a form of human organization can be explained by the fact that, given an adequate environment, internal competition contributed to domestic growth and yielded the lion's share of production surpluses to the ruling elite, who could thus afford the apparatus required to maintain domestic law and order. At the same time, growth and competition have provided unprecedented, though unevenly distributed, possibilities for human living: household conveniences, cheap and rapid communication and transportation devices, health facilities, entertainment at the flick of a switch.

On the other hand, competition has also constituted a threat, sometimes latent, to the stability of the state and to the well-being of many people, often as much to the moral and psychological integrity of the "haves" as to the economic and social subsistence of the "have nots." Largely because of competition, many states are seldom truly at peace but instead alternate between covert and overt modes of hostility. Similarly, by assuring unequal access to resources and unequal apportionment of the national product, competition sooner or later provides some members of a society with incentives for combining among themselves to unseat the establishment and perhaps reorder the political and economic structures. Vast bureaucratic complexes now enmesh millions of people in all the larger societies, and complicated hierarchies separate the rank-and-file individual from the milieux where plans are drawn up, power exercised, and resources moved and allocated. The individual in the band or tribe may have had a simplistic understanding of how nature operated, but the consequences of a mistake were soon, if not immediately, apparent, and he was an active and influential enough member of his society to understand its processes.

In earlier times nature tended to dominate human affairs, but now the impact of our activities on the planet is vastly greater than ever before and increasing every decade. Today we have reached a point where humanity itself is the principal determinant of the future of the planet. Suddenly, however, just as we are achieving unprecedented levels of technological development, a whole new array of problems seems to threaten us. Today there is accumulating evidence that growth and competition phenomena are sweeping us through a new transformation, the revolution of cybernetics and the massive impoundment and applications of mechanical energy.

The challenges to societies that emerge from competition and rapid growth can be serious enough, but when resource scarcities provide a compounding factor, some people fear that the implications may be catastrophic. Societies today are beginning to reach physical limitations on their activities. The implications of these limitations are far more devastating than those of other periods in which human beings have encountered them. Many societies in the past have confronted local scarcities, but now the whole planet is involved. On the one hand, we have more control over our environment than ever before. On the other, with the potent technologies available (including nuclear weaponry), the damage we can do to ourselves and our planet is unprecedented.

Earlier civilizations often solved their problems of scarce resources by expanding into a neighboring region or opening other parts of the world to commerce through exploration and charting of the seas. Today, when human demands are vastly greater, people are being forced to dig deeper, to find new uses for old resources, to draw upon the oceans as never before, to tap the sun in some way—even to consider tempering our demands. In the meantime, for our more immediate, day-to-day demands, the highly industrialized societies rely upon Third World countries for a large part of the resources required—at a time when those countries are themselves demanding more and often bending every effort to industrialize. As the Third World countries modernize, they will require increasing amounts of resources for their own enterprises. In the long run, spectacular new technological developments may make massive resources available, but for the immediate future such limitations will have to be confronted. Such a period of critical scarcities raises the specter of acute competition and widespread violence.

The Threat of Total Violence

Along with other organizational and technological phenomena, the institutions and weapons of warfare have undergone critical transformations since the Old Stone Age. It goes without saying that a modern war involves vastly more people and greater amounts of energy and other resources than our distant forebears could possibly have conceived of. In an even deeper time perspective, we contemplate the evolution of the human being, as envisioned by Konrad Lorenz in his book *On Aggression*, from dove to hawk, from "a basically harmless, omnivorous creature, lacking in natural weapons with which to kill his prey," to the largest-scale, most systematic, and effective killer on the planet.

Most important, the changes, while technological and organizational in their most obvious manifestations, have had their own consequences for human nature and values. Thus, as viewed by Lorenz, the distance at which all shooting weapons take effect has had the consequence of screening the killer from his victim, from those very elements that might otherwise stir his compassion and inhibit the killing. The outcome of technology has been that over time this critical distance has become greater and greater. In Lorenz's words, the "deep, emotional layers of our personality simply do not register the fact that the crooking of the forefinger to release a shot tears the entrails of another man." Even less, then, is the person who presses the release button of a bomb or ICBM capable of realizing, emotionally, the consequences of his action. Still more disturbing is the possibility that massive killing at a distance may so condition at least some members of a society to the idea of killing that killing face-to-face becomes easier for them. Increasingly, too, we confront the possibility of individuals and small terrorist groups substituting nuclear weapons for the more conventional bombs they are currently setting off.

If international relations and the behavior of states and empires were wholly congruent with this scenario, we might then expect a constant state of crisis and war. Obviously this is not the case, although at any given moment various individuals and small groups in the world are engaged in killing other people, and some number of countries in the world are likely to be in a state of crisis or war. The reason that human politics, economics, and warfare present such a mixed group of behaviors is simple, but fundamental: people are not robots, countries are not merely big machines, and neither domestic nor international affairs are mechanistic. Politics, economics, conflict, warfare, and all other essentially social activities are moved by human beings who have minds, emotions, values, memories, preferences, ambitions, and expectations and are thus partly rational, partly irrational—and always subject to change.

The growth, expansion, competitions, and conflicts of a society are all *human* undertakings which would not take place if people did not make them take place. But it is also true that *changes in both the natural environment and the social environment affect the way people think, feel, and act, just as the way people think, feel, and act affects the natural and social environments.* Thus, whatever we do to the natural and social environments today will affect the way we think, feel, and act tomorrow. This is how we shape the future bit by bit—often so slowly and imperceptibly that we altogether fail to perceive how the hard times befalling us are in large part of our own doing.

Historically, people have always tended to suffer severe stresses and strains as their societies have undergone system transformations. To the extent that the cybernetic and nuclear revolution becomes a full-blown reality, we may expect conflicts between old and new belief and behavior patterns and wrenching changes in human values and institutions. For the most part, human beings suffer discomfort when forced to deal with phenomena they cannot understand. Most societies include specialists who know more about the belief system and its values, explanations, rituals, and imperatives than other members, and in appropriate circumstances they are consulted or called upon to officiate. The trend since Paleolithic times has been from the shaman to the priest to the modern scientist. But often new technologies offer alternative explanations and alternate methods of response, thus challenging the traditional belief system and eroding the institutions that support it. Today, in large part because of the speed of technological and social change, virtually *all* beliefs and sources of authority are to some degree suspect.

Currently, through our population growth and rapidly advancing technologies, we appear to be impelling ourselves into a new revolution. The implications of this revolution are likely to be unprecedented. Due to increases in our numbers, our spiraling demands for resources, the speed of our communications, and the destructiveness of our weapons, we have shrunk the earth, relatively speaking, to a fraction of its ancient size. By thus altering our natural and social environments in massive yet sometimes quite subtle ways, we may also be altering ourselves without full awareness of what we are doing. Have our numbers and our mechanical knowledge and skills outstripped our wisdom and our sense of moral responsibility?

Today human beings seem to have reached an unprecedented decision point, a possible threshold for the transformation of human institutions and aspirations. Are we going to be enslaved, possibly even destroyed, by indiscriminate reliance upon our inventions? Or are we going to deepen our insights, broaden our horizons, strengthen our sense of responsibility for the long-term outcomes of our day-to-day activities?

The state, with its dependence on legitimized violence, is but a stage in human development and social organization. Since man's emergence as a species, human beings have lived in bands, tribes, or chiefdoms for all but a brief part of their existence. The state, with its characteristic values and institutions, is a comparatively recent invention. Neither human nature nor our form of social organization is fixed, immutable, or determined. This means that we are *not* locked into the present situation, that we can work toward the development of an alternate future. The important question is, what kind of future is most viable for mankind? As a tool to help us answer that question we will examine three utopian models of organization. They will help us to understand how states have operated in the past, how they respond to and shape human values, and how alternate forms and procedures might be developed for the future.

Man at the Crossroads by Diego Rivera.

Peaceable Kingdom by Edward Hicks.

CHAPTER FOUR

THREE UTOPIAS

IN THE EARLY PAGES of this book I suggested that utopias or abstract models of social systems can be used as yardsticks, so to speak, for measuring societies in the real world or as takeoff points for the generation of new alternatives. Utopia building can also be useful in helping us to identify our fundamental assumptions, to make our operational values more explicit, and to identify ways in which basic values conflict, short-term interests damage long-term interests, and so forth. I cautioned, however, that a great deal of damage can be done when people believe too dogmatically in their utopias.

In this chapter we will examine three models, or utopias—a "tooth and claw" or unrestrained competition model, a competition-welfare model, and a multilevel, equal-access model—which derive from quite different perspectives and interpretations of human prehistory and history. It is unlikely that any real-world society has ever resembled closely any one of these models, but most features of each model have some identifiable precedents. More important, the three models taken together provide reference points in terms of which almost any real-world society or projection of the future can be located, described, and assessed. And most important of all, perhaps, a consideration of these three models may help each of us to ascertain what his own assumptions about human nature and human potentials really are, what his deepest held values are, and what values—under pressure—he is willing to relinquish or trade off in favor of some other perceived gain or preferred outcome.

An Unrestrained Competition or Tooth and Claw Model

Many different models could be derived from the fundamental assumptions that individual human beings and even classes and races differ genetically in their capabilities and potentials; that such inherent differences create a certain amount of inequality, competition, domination, compliance, and even exploitation that is not only unavoidable but even desirable; and that human progress depends, in the long run, upon the prominence, superior influence, and survival of the most capable people. Among the many possible models, however, one has been widely developed. This unrestrained competition model was developed during the late nineteenth and early twentieth centuries by writers who had been strongly influenced by Charles Darwin's theory of evolution. These writers placed great emphasis upon the biological aspects of human development as distinguished from processes of socialization and the human capacity for learning from past experience. Human prehistory and history were largely interpreted on this basis, and the resulting inferences and conclusions were then applied to contemporary problems not only by the neo-Darwinian writers themselves but also by a great many politicians, statesmen, and other public figures.

In contrast to the neo-Darwinian approach, Marxism-Leninism and Maoism present an alternate set of unrestrained competition models that emphasize technological and economic (as opposed to genetic) determinism. Within these models, changes in the forces of production create new divisions of labor and generate fundamental contradictions between classes in a society. These contradictions, in turn, give rise to class struggles which are the motive force of social development and overall human progress.

Much of the language and many of the basic ideas of the neo-Darwinists now seem out of date, somewhat unsavory, even reprehensible. Yet if we consider the assumptions, hypotheses, and doctrines seriously, they will remind us of many arguments put forward in somewhat different language today. Recent claims of genetically controlled racial differences in basic intelligence offer one example.

Some people may even find themselves in more agreement with neo-Darwinist assumptions than they might have anticipated. Darwinian theory implied that the natural relationship between organisms and groups of organisms was one of competition for survival. Numerous efforts have been made to incorporate this perspective into explanations of social, cultural, political, and economic development, but so-called neo-Darwinian approaches have been distinguished from others by their strong (and many critics would say far too narrow) focus upon the process of natural selection in organic evolution. As understood during much of the nineteenth century, the Darwinian concept of natural selection emphasized "the struggle for existence" and "the survival of the fittest."

The long course of human biological evolution was perceived as causing, or at least making possible, our use of language, tools, and other cultural achievements—almost to the exclusion of our capacities for social learning and autonomous conceptualization, for projection of new ideas into the future, and for planned change. Associated with this emphasis was a tendency to consider members of advanced cultures as biologically superior to members of more primitive ones and members of the upper classes as innately superior to members of the lower classes. Human innovation, progress, and civilization were viewed in biological rather than in psychological or social terms. Social organization thus was believed to be biologically determined in much the same way as the growth of the embryo or the unfolding of a flower, and heavy emphasis was placed upon the effect of human organization and custom upon the genetic stock. Competition was accepted as a law of nature which could no more be done away with than gravitation, and which human beings could ignore only to their sorrow. Progress was viewed as dependent upon the selection process, which emerged, in turn, from unrestricted competition.

If we view human development within this framework, it becomes self-evident that the less fit varieties of human being will be eliminated or subordinated, regardless of the source of variations, and the more fit will be maintained. Human beings thus have no other recourse than to resign themselves to struggle in a world where only the fit survive and the weak go to the wall. Under nature's laws all people alike are put on trial. Certain human qualities, even moral attributes, are inherently more conducive to adaptive, basic, and desirable change, with the result that evolution proceeds along more or less predetermined lines. Freedom and justice in an unrestrained competition model thus amount to the right of the fit to prevail over the unfit. "If we do not like the survival of the fittest," declared William Graham Sumner, a leading neo-Darwinian theorist, "we have only one possible alternative, and that is survival of the unfittest. The former is the law of civilization; the latter is the law of anti-civilization."

There are rough parallels between neo-Darwinian doctrine and Marxist-Leninist theory with respect to the inevitability of competition and conflict between major components of a society. In modern times, however, the fit and progressive neo-Darwinian elements in society are the great capitalists and other rich and powerful magnates, whereas the downtrodden—the poor peasants and the proletarians—are the fit and progressive classes in Marxist-Leninist and Maoist theory.

The doctrine of brutal competition, conflict, struggle, and survival of the fittest, according to its proponents, is not only realistic, correct, and scientifically true, it is also *just* and *right*. During the late nineteenth and early twentieth centuries the doctrine of competition and survival of the fittest was used in the United States and other Western countries to justify a whole range of domestic and foreign undertakings that were sometimes challenged as exploitative. People who have met their responsibilities in the world cannot be considered equal to those who have not. Hence, inequalities of status and class are reflections of differences in moral fiber and social fitness.

In the great struggle for existence, money is the token of success and the surest measure of virtue. Whenever rivals are after the means of subsistence from nature, Sumner explains, "the one who has capital has immeasurable advantages over the other." But accumulations of capital can be achieved only by self-denial, and, he continues, "if possession of it did not secure advantages and superiorities of a high order men would never submit to what is necessary to get it." Millionaires, political leaders, magnates, warlords, and conquerors are in control because they have demonstrated themselves to be of superior stock. The poor, the starving, and the helpless, on the other hand, are weak precisely because they are inferior. Might does indeed make right. The poor are unfit and should be eliminated. "The whole effort of nature is to get rid of such," Herbert Spencer declared, "to clear the world of them, and make room for better." Social welfare legislation, by encouraging the unfit to reproduce, weakens the human race.

During the late nineteenth and early twentieth centuries spokesmen for the doctrine of unrestrained competition and survival of the fittest generally applied it more evenly (to private enterprise as well as to economic classes and individuals) than some of their theoretical and practical successors today:

> "Professor, don't you believe in any government aid to industries?" a student asked of William Graham Sumner.
> "No!" replied Sumner, "It's root, hog, or die."
> "Yes, but hasn't the hog got a right to root?"
> "There are no rights. The world owes nobody a living."

From Sumner's perspective, there was no more reason for pampering an inefficient firm than for helping an incompetent individual.

Charge of Police by Umberto Boccioni.

During recent years, with increasing concern for scarcities of food, water, oil, and other critical materials, a great deal of attention has been focused upon how such resources are (and should be) allocated among the peoples of the world: who should get what, how, when, and how much? Insofar as they draw upon the world's declining supply of food and other critical resources, according to Garrett Hardin, the "poor" and "improvident" assume less than their share of responsibility for protecting the earth than do the rich and provident who are manning the lifeboat for survival. If aided by the rich, the poor will only increase their numbers further and swamp the lifeboat. Famine should be viewed as one of nature's ways of telling improvident and profligate peoples that they have been irresponsible in their living habits.

Contemporary "lifeboat ethics" depart from strict neo-Darwinism in that they allow for a certain amount of social learning among the "improvident." If each country were held solely responsible for its own well-being, according to Hardin, the poorly managed ones would suffer. But they could learn from experience, mend their ways, and thus work more effectively to solve their basic problems.

Social Darwinists saw battlefields as the ultimate testing grounds of cultures, states, empires, and whole civilizations. As social, political, and economic struggle raises the fittest to leadership in the domestic arena, so in the world at large international conflict and violence separate the weak and degenerate races and nationalities from the progressive and strong, thus benefiting the species. However much any of us might regret the horrors and the suffering of warfare, argued the Social Darwinists, we must accept it as a source of social advancement. "When races stop struggling," Lester Ward wrote in a 1905 discussion of war, "progress ceases." From this we may infer that the "just war" for the neo-Darwinist is likely to involve the defense by the progressive rich, the developed, and the "fit" of their territory, their markets and trade routes, their access to critical resources, and, under appropriate circumstances, the aggressive extension of their power and interests. This perspective can be contrasted with the Maoist concept of the just war, which is fought against the rich, the powerful, and the exploitative by the progressive poor and dispossessed. For the Maoist, progress ceases when classes stop struggling and when the colonies and semicolonies, such as post-World War II Vietnam, are unable to oppose imperialist expansion.

From ancient times states and empires approximating the unrestrained competition model have left their mark on human civilization, culture, and "progress." The ruins of their roads, temples, palaces, pyramids, and monuments still remain, and their contributions to engineering and mathematics, art and literature cannot be overlooked. Few people would deny, however that many of these remarkable achievements were accomplished at incalculable human cost.

A Competition-Welfare Model

The competition-welfare approach shares certain broad premises with the unrestrained competition model: human beings differ in their capabilities and dispositions. In considerable part because of these differences, competition in human affairs is inevitable. Additionally, however, in this model competition is seen as desirable because it disciplines various participants in economic life and provides them with incentives for producing goods and services skillfully, efficiently, and cheaply. It is thus by way of competition that societies develop in ways that ensure progress and yield the material, social, psychological, and perhaps even spiritual, resources and benefits that people require and expect.

Underlying the competition-welfare model is the basic assumption that whereas individuals differ in terms of their potentials and disabilities, neither of these is necessarily genetically controlled, nor is either always measurable or otherwise ascertainable. Variations in basic capability occur in terms of individuals, not whole classes, nationalities, or races. All human beings should thus be provided with equal opportunities for self-improvement. Because of individual differences, some people will rise to positions of greater power, responsibility, influence, and reward than others; but all human beings should be provided with a floor or baseline sufficient to guarantee their fundamental survival and welfare. (In theory, at least, Western democratic countries tend to view all citizens, whatever their individual differences, as equal before the law, whereas Communist countries are more vocal about economic equality. In fact, both of these concepts tend to be honored more in profession than in practice.)

The competition-welfare approach recognizes various minimal rights, freedoms, and expectations to which each person may lay claim merely because he or she is a human being. Included among these are certain fundamental legal rights and safeguards, certain rights of opportunity, and certain rights, usually ill-defined, to minimal subsistence and welfare. The emphasis within the competition-welfare approach, generally, is upon equality of opportunity for individual human beings at the doorway of life, but gross inequality in the distribution of outcomes. Such conceptualizations of restraint upon pure competition open the way, in the competition-welfare approach, to redefinitions of and a self-conscious concern for various fundamental problems of freedom, justice, and equality. How free is an individual or how useful the right to vote if he or she earns a wage that falls below subsistence or suffers chronic unemployment?

In his book *A Theory of Justice*, legal theorist John Rawls proposed that all social value—"liberty and opportunity, income and wealth, and the bases of self-respect"—should be distributed equally in a just society unless an unequal distribution of some of these values would be to everyone's advantage. But such inequalities are justified, according to Rawls, only when the greater prospects allowed to the more advantaged members of society encourage them to do things that raise the long-term prospects of the disadvantaged. Unequal distributions may be justifiable, for example, when they motivate entrepreneurs to make economic processes more efficient, to speed innovation, and so on. Eventually, Rawls notes, the resulting material benefits may spread throughout the system and reach the least advantaged.

If the distribution of goods within a society is governed by a variable such as individual capability or merit, then differentials in distribution may be expected to contribute to competition. The practical difficulty is that the inequalities that are allowed within a society (and often between societies as well) fail to enhance everybody's advantage. Or, more precisely, the usual tendency in a growing, competitive society is that the standard of living available to everybody does indeed rise, but the gaps between levels of advantage remain essentially the same. The more productive and prosperous people often improve their comparative advantage by increasing amounts. While the rich and powerful become even richer and more powerful, the middle and lower-middle levels tend to be caught in never-ending competitions that fail to advance their relative standing in any significant way. Meanwhile, people on the bottommost levels either sink into relative poverty or, in modern welfare societies, become less and less productive and more and more dependent on handouts. The arrangements of the society do not provide them with even the most minimal leverage necessary if they are to invest in themselves and thus become more productive and self-sufficient.

These outcomes often run counter to the professed values that seem to prevail in the society—values pertaining to individual rights and equal opportunity, for example. Thus, the ready conclusion among many of the more efficient, productive, and prosperous citizens is that the less successful are in some way morally deficient. From this perspective, people are successful and free in different degrees according to their states of mind and competence; the unsuccessful remain where they are because of a lack of ambition or because of some other flaw in their characters.

According to the competition-welfare model, economic logic demands some degree of economic inequality, even in the face of political egalitarianism. Indeed, institutionalized inequalities—inequalities between classes by income and wealth—which affect people's whole life prospects are inescapable. But this reality is not seen as undesirable for it also provides incentives such that the economy is more efficient, industrial advance proceeds at a quicker pace, and so on. The end result is that greater material and other benefits are distributed throughout the system.

From this viewpoint, the future of a society that is efficient and growing but also free and just depends on the preservation of beliefs that give room to "creative inequalities." A society is thus expected to guarantee welfare without damaging initiative, provide security without undermining incentives, maintain stability without imposing regimentation, encourage change without courting disruption or discontinuity.

Within the competition-welfare approach, the seeming contradictions between efficiency and welfare and between inequality and justice have normally been solved by increasing productivity and thus providing absolute increases in income to all classes, but allowing the proportional share of the upper groups to remain relatively undisturbed. In principle, taxes restrain the concentration of income at the top while employment and upward pressure on wages increase well-being at the bottom, although "loopholes" at upper-income levels frequently abort the redistribution effort. In addition, specialized "giveaway" institutions are created in order to achieve some further redistributions of goods and services and in order to maintain a minimal level of subsistence and welfare. But unlike giveaway institutions in bands, tribes, and even chiefdoms, where the transfer from donor to receiver is direct, modern states tend to build large and complex hierarchies of paid giveaway specialists. As a consequence, in private and public giveaway bureaucracies alike, it may cost a great many dollars to give one dollar away. By eliminating the more acute tensions associated with inequality, increased production thus serves as an alternative to radical redistribution.

Contemporary societies even remotely approximating the competition-welfare model confront serious difficulties. In the United States and a number of other countries during recent decades, competition among large and powerful enterprises has often been minimized, if not eliminated, through price fixing, governmental subsidies, and comparable mechanisms which protect less efficient firms—often at the expense of consumers or taxpayers. At the same time, economic growth, greater concentrations of wealth, and the social conditions of highly industrialized and predominantly urban societies have generated demands for welfare measures that were scarcely dreamed of a few decades back. In the world of today and tomorrow many demands that in an earlier era could be met in other, often simpler ways now seem to call for special arrangements. Temporarily unemployed workers cannot go home to the farm and live off the land anymore; they need unemployment compensation. The aged can no longer plan to live with their children; they need social security and a retirement plan. Medical protection no longer consists of simple remedies prescribed by a kindly country doctor and available for a few cents; our higher standards call for hospitalization insurance and other forms of protection. Industrial workers, farmers, teachers, policemen, firemen, retired people—almost all of us—want a larger share of the national product and are more inclined to demand it.

The competition-welfare model can be applied not only to individual countries but also to certain aspects of the international environment where successful countries compete for resources, markets, spheres of influence, political power, and strategic advantage while at the same time extending economic and technological assistance to some of the poorer nations. Over recent generations states and empires approximating the competition-welfare model have provided much of the genius, management, labor, and capital not only for the industrialization and modernization of their own societies but also for the growth of less-developed nations. Indeed, until very recently, such states and empires have been viewed by many people as the most promising instruments for solving basic human problems and for providing people everywhere with new possibilities for welfare and self-fulfillment. All too frequently, however, the United States and other powerful industrialized states, while raising living standards at home and creating higher expectations everywhere, have been much less successful with their development programs in the poorer countries. The rich nations still tend to become richer and the poor nations poorer. Often, too, the well-to-do classes in poor countries benefit from such aid programs while the poverty stricken sink even lower.

In certain ways, countries as different in their social, economic, and political systems as the United States and the Soviet Union may approximate the competition-welfare model. Generally, the emphasis in this country has been to constrain political competition more than economic competition. Consequently, the U.S. citizen may feel that economic insecurities have undermined his own political security and influence, while economically powerful interests dominate politics and shape much of his life-style. In contrast, a citizen of the USSR may discover that political insecurities have limited his social and economic gains.

A Multilevel, Equal-Access Model

The multilevel, equal-access model derives from the idea that human beings, like all other creatures on earth, are parts of nature, not masters over it, and are subject to nature's laws. No individual, group, or nation properly holds title to the earth and its resources, but merely enjoys use of it for a period of time. From this premise it follows that unequal access to and unequal distributions of resources and other earthly benefits are arbitrary arrangements created by human beings and without natural justification. This model also assumes that social stability, as well as justice, is enhanced to the extent that a gain or loss of the society as a whole is shared as equally as possible by all the individual members.

In social, political, and economic terms there are three basic points of reference for human affairs: the planet and its resources as a whole, mankind as a whole, and the individual person. All human organizations and groupings between the individual person and mankind at large are arrangements created by people primarily in order to sustain, regulate, and manage relations among themselves and with the natural environment. Within this framework, the fundamental, natural, and irreducible human unit is the individual person who in very basic ways comes into the world alone and departs it alone.

The individual human being is a fundamental unit in the unrestrained competition model and the competition-welfare model because the capabilities of the individual are perceived as determining where he or she fits into the societal structure and how he or she is rewarded or penalized. In the multilevel, equal-access model, however, the individual is the irreducible unit of all human affairs because groups and organizations are mere arrangements of individuals, and *only* the individual can feel, perceive, remember, expect, project, and decide. For these reasons, if for no other, each individual has a natural right to live, think, act, pursue personal interests, and be protected from exploitation, injury, and other abuse *subject only to the equivalent claim of every other person to similar rights and protections.* The basic legal test in any controversy between parties is the extent to which either might gain or lose advantage or protection if their roles or positions were reversed.

Everything pertaining to the individual is affected by interactions with the physical environment, with people, and with other living creatures. This means that what I do to you today will be motivated and shaped, in part at least, not only by what I did to you yesterday, but also by what you did to me yesterday. Thus, each of us is partly responsible for the other's behavior and plight. When the case of *The*

People v. *John Doe* comes to court, the plaintiff is in a sense on trial along with the defendant.

Competition is recognized within the multilevel, equal-access model as a phenomenon of nature, but cooperation is perceived as being equally real and pervasive among living creatures. The two need not be mutually exclusive. The "tooth and claw" perception of nature is thus one-sided and inaccurate. In fact, cooperation and competition tend to be played out interactively among subhuman species as well as among people. There is ample evidence from the Paleolithic Age up to the present that human beings have a special genius for cooperation when they choose to use it. Hence, from this perspective, the basic issues are *what kinds of competition*—for what purposes and on what levels—combined with *what kinds of cooperation* will best serve human as well as planetary needs now and in the future.

This approach recognizes that human beings differ widely. It presumes, however, that if the abilities and limitations of numbers of people are taken into account, many of the differences in aptitude will tend to balance out, with some individuals scoring higher in certain talents, others in capacities of another sort. In addition, what appear to be basic differences in individual capacities are often the outcome of quite differential experiences and environmental influences shaping one's development. As capitalism's great genius Adam Smith pointed out some 200 years ago in his book *The Wealth of Nations*, the "difference of natural talents in different men is, in reality, much less than we are aware of, and the very genius which appears to distinguish men of different professions, when grown to maturity, is not so much the cause as the effect of the division of labor." The differences that seem to distinguish the pauper, the king, and the philosopher may arise less from nature than from personal background, experience, opportunity, and even random fortune.

Human differences emerge from a variety of human sources, many of which cannot be avoided. A considerable number, however, are the result of unequal access to, and unequal distributions of, resources and benefits. Such differences are attributable to conditions that are not "natural" or "inevitable" but are essentially human artifacts and therefore subject to change. "Wherever there is great property," wrote Adam Smith, "there is great inequality," and therefore great differences in perspective, values, goals, expectations, and behaviors. This tends to be true of societies irrespective of their particular political systems. Whatever the political and legal guarantees of justice in the abstract, it is unlikely that people with substantially unequal access to resources, even in a so-called socialist society, will obtain equally just outcomes. Justice therefore requires that during his or her lifetime each person should enjoy a right to resources and a share in the total human enterprise equal to that of every other living person on the planet—with equal responsibility for care of the resources so held in trust. Any system of justice founded on any other distribution of access and rights is flawed at its base.

From this perspective, equal individual access to resources can contribute to stability as well as to justice. As viewed by Adam Smith, it is

> only under the shelter of the civil magistrate that the owner of that valuable property, which is acquired by the labor of many years, or perhaps of many successive generations, can sleep a single night in security. He is at all times surrounded by unknown enemies whom, though he never provoked, he can never appease, and from whose injustice he can be protected only by the powerful arm of the civil magistrate continually held up to chastise it.

But, he continues, "where there is no property"—as among Stone Age bands and tribes—"or at least none that exceeds the value of two or three days' labor, civil government is not so necessary."

In any society, revolutionary participation, criminal activities, and other types of deviant behavior are likely to correlate with the degree to which critical social, economic, political, and related problems confronting the people remain unsolved and also with the degree to which legitimate means of altering the situation or otherwise relieving the tension are blocked. From city ghetto to the international system the greater the blockage, through whatever circumstances, the higher the levels of violence and other pathological phenomena to be expected.

Within an equal-access framework, the interests of the individual and the group are closely aligned: any improvement in the general welfare will mean an improvement in the situation of the individual, but no individual will gain at the expense of another; and any decline in the general welfare of a society will be felt more or less simultaneously *and equally* by all.

Some Institutional Characteristics of the Equal-Access Model

Since to date no society on a state level has organized itself along the lines of the multilevel, equal-access model, we can best understand its implications, perhaps, if we consider some of the values and institutional mechanisms that might be required if such a system were ever to function.

Both political and economic institutions within this framework operate to keep differences in access to resources and benefits within relatively narrow limits. The pursuit, maintenance, and regulation of all human affairs and enterprises are carried out on a variety of levels and within many different jurisdictions including the family, the neighborhood, the community, the province, the nation, the region, and the world. As many decisions as functionally possible are made at the individual, family, and community levels. Only those decisions that cannot be carried out effectively at the local level are delegated to a higher level. Whenever the appropriate level of jurisdiction is in doubt, the presumption will favor the lower level.

The ultimate locus of political sovereignty is the individual. Consonant with his or her solemn responsibility as an equally empowered trustee for and shareholder in the planet and its resources, no individual may relinquish or be required to forfeit his basic personal sovereignty, though he may assign limited proxy rights to representatives and public executives on various levels of regulation and governance. Such assignments of proxy are limited in time and are for specific functions. In any instance of ambiguity, the presumption is clear that the official possesses no more authority than the individuals within his jurisdiction have specifically granted to him.

Lawmakers and executives are chosen by election, lot, rotation, or by a combination of these procedures. The method of selection is that which is deemed most effective and appropriate for the level and the particular office to be filled. For example, a panel of candidates may be selected from the public at large and the lawmaker or public executive chosen from the panel by election. The combining of election with lot and rotation should help to inhibit the development of entrenched lobbies, discourage the establishment of powerful political machines, and strengthen the political influence of the people at large. At first glance such procedures may seem risky, but they are not new. Ancient Athens, medieval and early Renaissance Florence, and many other societies have used lot and rotation mechanisms for selecting their representatives, and today the outcome of civil suits and even the fate of a person on trial for a capital offense may be decided by a jury selected by a combination of processes.

An individual is liable to the extent that he or she violates the inalienable rights and protections of another person. It is a violation, for instance, to accept more than one's per capita share of resources or of gross product from the total human enterprise. Within this framework, an individual who profits at the expense of other people has committed a violation much as if he or she had stolen from them. Minor infractions are taxable, the proceeds being awarded, where appropriate, as compensation to the injured parties or absorbed by the public treasury. Gross or repeated infractions render the perpetrator subject to rehabilitation carried out by designated institutions seeking to help the perpetrator prepare for and find a role in society that is rewarding and that does not threaten the social, economic, or political well-being of other people.

Those who make the laws in an equal-access society are selected for varying but restricted tenures to establish and maintain the values and goals of human affairs and enterprises on the various levels. Public executives, also selected for varying but restricted tenures, are responsible for administering public functions within the mandated legal framework at their operating level. Both representatives and public executives are subject to recall for malfeasance or abuse of power.

Within this framework equal access to information is as important as equal access to material resources. Those who seek power normally require resources, and those who possess or control resources tend to wield power. But the ability to use resources effectively depends also upon the ability to organize and communicate. In this respect, information may be viewed as a resource: whoever controls information is likely to enjoy some measure of power. Unequal access to information thus contributes to hierarchies of power, and to the extent that *A* possesses secret information about *B* (even false information, so long as it is not subject to challenge or critical assessment), to that extent *A* tends to have arbitrary power over *B*. In this model, sources of information are plural and competitive with one another at all levels, and all data collections, pools, and archives are subject to public inspection.

The basic unit of work is the person-hour, the value of which derives from the consideration that it is an hour of a human being's life. Therefore, each person-hour has the same value as every other person-hour. As much as possible, work loads are equally shared—with minor variations according to the requirements of particular localities, industries, trades, and professions. Bonuses in the form of immediately consumable goods or services are granted to people who do particularly hazardous, onerous, or unpleasant work. No individual who does more than his share of work can gain any fundamental economic advantage therefrom, but he or she may receive an *ad hoc* reward in terms of special vacation expenses or some other immediately consumable bonus. Work is available for every person who wants it, and every effort is made to train people in the fields in which they have an interest and are sufficiently qualified. People who do not work may still draw their share of subsistence, health care, and the like. But travel, entertainment, and luxuries of any kind are obtainable only by those who have done their share of work. In general, any major gain to the society as a whole is shared equally by all its people. Thus surplus profits from highly efficient enterprises are normally used to improve the environment and general welfare of the community that manages them. Beyond certain thresholds, however, a portion of the surplus created by a more productive society is invested for the improvement of production in a less productive society.

Among engineers it is common practice to design complex systems in terms of inverse feedbacks. This means that a part of the output of a component system is used in a way that will either reduce the output of that system or increase the input to a competitive component within the same enterprise. Such an arrangement serves as a regulator to keep competition within bounds—to prevent one system from overproducing and another from underproducing in a way that may be damaging to the overall enterprise. Among hunting and gathering bands and tribes a variety of giveaway rituals performed this function.

Some years back, the motion picture *Edison, the Man* demonstrated the basic kind of problem that can be regulated by inverse feedback arrangements. The picture showed Spencer Tracy, as Edison, trying to turn valves and throw switches fast enough to control two generators in a positive feedback, or runaway, situation. Confronted by an unmanageable system, Edison, with more practicality than finesse, installed a heavy shaft and some large gears that forced the two generators to turn at the same speed. This arrangement worked, after a fashion, but there was a more sophisticated and efficient solution involving inverse feedbacks that he did not perceive at the time. This involves the transfer of part of the load from one generator to the other: if the first generator picks up excess energy, it shifts the overflow to the other generator, which takes it up.

The Edison story may provide us with a useful parable, for social systems are shot through with positive feedbacks in runaway conditions—population growth, arms production, inflation, pollution, and the depletion of certain critical resources, to mention only a few. And runaway competitions, among states and also among competing economic sectors or competing classes and interest groups within states, are roughly comparable to Edison's runaway generator system. But perhaps even more notable, Edison's *forced solution*, the installation of the heavy shaft and large gears, may be viewed as crudely analogous to the coercive methods used by some societies in order to compel a regulation of the competitions that naturally arise from differences in capabilities and efficiencies.

Each production enterprise in a multilevel, equal-access society is organized and operated cooperatively by those who are served by it. Profits (or losses) are declared at appropriate intervals and are shared by the community of participants—with the promise that profits above a subsistence threshold are taxed at a decelerating rate, the proceeds being diverted to other desirable but less profitable enterprises according to the principles of inverse feedback. But if growth is to be discouraged, the tax rate may be accelerated.

Some inverse feedback arrangements already operate within competition-welfare frameworks (e.g., transfer payments), but they tend to be partial and not fully rationalized. Transfer payments within an equal-access model can be used to restrict disruptive positive feedback in a society, to prevent execssive growth, or to equalize production or consumption between two or more groups in a society. Or they can be used to keep two or more activities within a society operating according to some desired ratio.

In this model, inverse feedback also operates as a basic regulating and equilibrating mechanism whereby a profitable enterprise assists in the establishment of a new enterprise; or a profitable enterprise, damaging to the environment, uses its profits to restore the environment; or a useful but damaging enterprise (freeway system) is taxed to support a useful, less damaging enterprise (mass transit). Wherever possible, such capital transfers will be used to serve investment rather than welfare functions. For example, a profit-making community supports a program to provide training for people who would otherwise be unemployable, or to help them establish their own undertakings; or it invests in an enterprise that will put a weak community on its feet, rather than merely subsidizing it.

In view of the world's large and ever-increasing population, the complexity of technology, and the enormous resource demands being made today, it is not at all evident that anything like the multilevel, equal-access model could ever be established or maintained. At this stage in human development, at least, a major purpose of this model is to provide—along with the unrestrained competition model and the competition-welfare model—a tool for assessing real-world societies as they operate today and for guiding the development of alternative social, political, and economic institutions that might be useful in the future. The challenge is how to harness the ideas and tools of the fifth great system break, the revolution of cybernation and the application of massive amounts of energy, in ways that will solve some of the severe problems created by that revolution and at the same time open up new possibilities for human fulfillment.

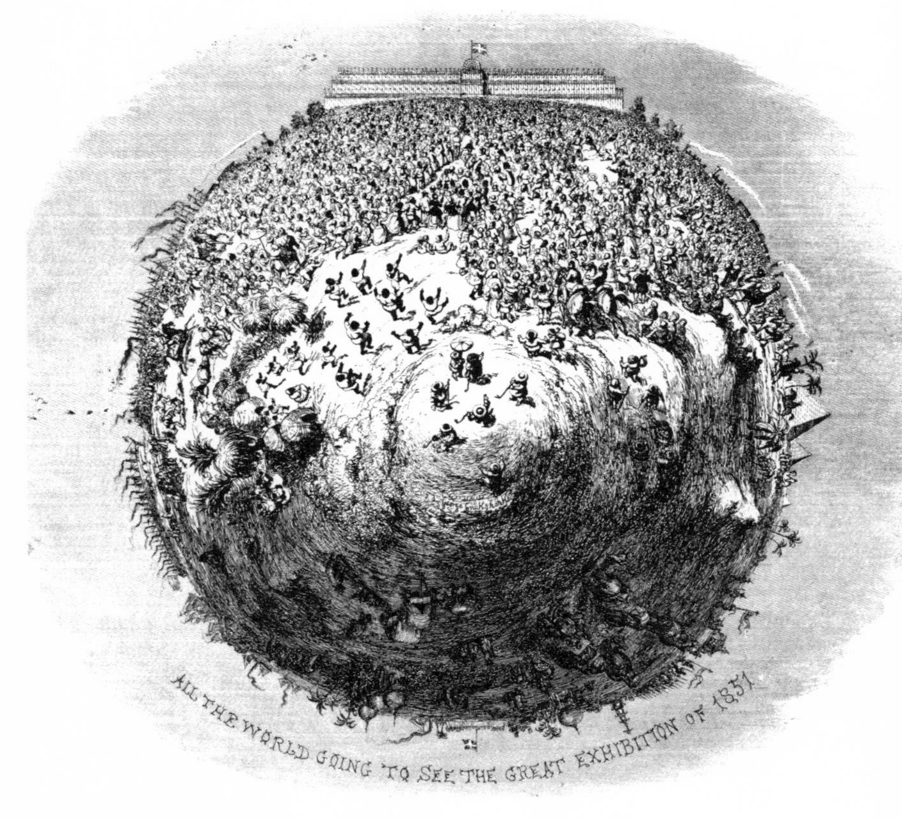

All The World Going to See The Great Exhibition of 1851 by George Cruikshank.

CHAPTER FIVE

CONFRONTING THE FUTURE

SOME OF THE ADVANTAGES and vulnerabilities of the unrestrained competition model, the competition-welfare model, and the multilevel, equal-access model are easily identified. Historically, states and empires approximating the unrestrained competition model have provided earlier civilizations with the bureaucratic organization, coercive power, and economic discipline to accomplish great feats. Their kings, pharaohs, and emperors ruled large populations and extensive territories. Using relatively simple tools, draft animals, and large gangs of slave or corvée labor, such societies built roads, defensive walls, canals, temples, palaces and imperial monuments which, in many instances, have survived and excite our wonder to this day. But the concept of human rights scarcely existed, and the notion of equality was scoffed at if conceived of at all. Laws normally favored the powerful rather than the weak, and justice was commonly defined in terms of "might makes right," being meted out according to the injured party's capacity for exacting restitution. Minor transgressions by the slave or the common man were often punished by torture or death.

As steam power—and later electrical power and the technology of the internal combustion engine—provided unprecedented ways to harness mechanical energy, slave labor and untutored gang labor in virtually all forms became less efficient and economical and were eventually replaced. Societies approximating the competition-welfare model developed ways of educating and conditioning new types of labor on all levels of enterprise, not only factory workers but also appropriately trained and motivated foremen, supervisors, engineers, accountants, purchasing agents, salesmen, managers, legal and financial experts, and so on. Equally important, such societies produced the incentives and institutions which, to a large extent, made the industrial revolution possible. The profit motive, investment institutions, cost-accounting techniques, banking mechanisms, and tax structures facilitated the concentration of capital and the financing of colossal enterprises. Our modern jetliners lacing the earth and our expeditions to the moon are only two of the more recent manifestations of what modern competition-welfare systems have been able to achieve.

Within a competition-welfare framework many of the more direct brutalities of intense competition have been eliminated or at least tempered by welfare arrangements. The unemployed, the weak, the sick, and the incompetent need not starve, even though they are unproductive. States and empires characterized by competition-welfare arrangements have achieved some of the most spectacular economic, political, and social advances in human history, but they have also committed some of the most brutal atrocities. Over the last two or three centuries Britain, France, the United States, Canada, Australia, the Netherlands, Germany, Italy, Japan, Russia in its own way, and even Nazi Germany and Fascist Italy have had much in common with the competition-welfare model. Only a few countries such as Norway, Sweden, Denmark, and New Zealand have so moderated competition and so developed welfare functions that they could be viewed as having possibly moved beyond this model.

In advanced industrial societies, and in developing countries as well, many people have come to believe that future technologies and competition tempered by welfare can provide virtually anything human beings demand. Even the so-called socialist countries rely heavily on technology and economic growth to solve current problems and to achieve a classless society.

Such confidence may be ill-founded, however. Today many of the most technologically advanced societies are plagued by inflation, depression, resource scarcities, pollution, burdensome taxes, unemployment, rising crime, clogged courts, and ugly ghettos. Most of these problems are related in complex ways: curbs on pollution restrict the extraction of badly needed resources; an attack on inflation increases unemployment. But neither the interrelationships nor the problems themselves are well understood.

A critical insight has emerged with the observation that growth itself, or at least unrestrained and nonselective growth, can create major problems in terms of environmental damage, depletion of resources, economic instabilities, exacerbated competition, and conflict worldwide. These possibilities, including that of an earth inhabited by more and more people competing for food, water, energy, and other resources in scarcer supply, are emerging precisely at a time when societies are building unprecedented systems of mass abuse and destruction. One of the basic laws of the universe involves the trade-off principle; that is, it is becoming more and more evident that virtually every "improvement," every new milestone of progress, is achieved at some very basic cost.

From today's perspective, the main usefulness of the multilevel, equal-access model may be that it serves to throw into sharp relief some of the problems that appear to be endemic in many contemporary societies approximating the competition-welfare model. But like other utopias, there are no guarantees in the equal-access model. We cannot be sure that any such society could be achieved or, if it were, that it could maintain itself. There is no certainty that multilevel, equal-access arrangements would satisfy large numbers of people or, if they did, that special interests would not subvert the new system. Not only does such a society not exist, but to many people today it may appear to be a simpleminded fantasy. Yet we might remind ourselves that over three million years or more of human development, large numbers of prestate societies have approximated the equal-access, democratic-participation aspects of this model and that the rapid drift away from it during the last few thousand years can be explained to a large extent by two major considerations: 1) the vastly greater numbers of people and 2) massive changes in their technological capabilities. These two trends are likely to persist well into the future.

New Perspectives on the Planning and Operation of Social Systems

As indicated in previous chapters, there is nothing sacred about these three models or any other utopia for that matter. Here they are presented only as tools for the design of alternate futures. But we cannot begin to use them until we identify a certain number of problems that contribute to our difficulties in preparing for tomorrow, next week, and further into the future.

The latter half of the twentieth century has been characterized by a new revolution or system break that may require new ways of doing things. Just as slave and other forms of gang labor became inefficient during the industrial revolution, present-day arrangements of capital and labor may become outdated. Computers, cybernetic control systems, and possibilities for harnessing unprecedented amounts of mechanical energy may make the competition-welfare type of labor force obsolete and with it our contemporary carrot-and-stick incentives. We need to begin thinking in wholly new terms. The problems many societies confront today—from inflation, pollution, and resource scarcities to bureaucratic ineptness, monetary crises, and urban terrorism—may be harbingers of coming change.

Fortunately our experiences of the past and present can be used to shape the future in significant ways. By constructing various kinds of utopias, we can deepen our understanding of the flaws that characterize existing institutions and prepare tentative blueprints for new possibilities. We cannot eliminate uncertainty in human affairs by this or any other method, but we can obtain a much better understanding of ourselves and of our potential for working with one another creatively. To some extent such basic thinking, experimentation, and consideration of future alternatives is already being undertaken by scholars and other specialists from a number of disciplines, but the participation of people from many walks of life is badly needed.

The Need for Social Learning

In this era of resource scarcities, some of the costs of rapid economic growth have become evident in inflation, energy crises, economic instability, and faltering political regimes in various parts of the industrialized world. The world's abundance-oriented systems, therefore, require reevaluation and revision. The contemporary system break may require that we replace many assumptions and rules of the past with new understandings and policies. This is likely to involve complex social learning on the part of many different societies. Yet how can we deal with our future, and that of our children and grandchildren, when we have so few satisfactory explanations for the past, such limited understanding of ourselves, and no crystal ball—not even a good telescope—for looking ahead?

No country is immune to the dangerous side effects of indiscriminate growth. Despite ideological differences, the social and economic strategies and goals of the United States, the Soviet Union, China, Japan, Germany, England, Mexico, Brazil, Nigeria, Iran, and most other countries are in one respect basically similar: they all promote activities that increase per capita use of resources, allow population growth, emphasize productivity, encourage economic expansion, and generate rising demands.

Fortunately a major insight which may be drawn from the preceding chapters is that human events do not just happen. They are not unavoidably determined or inevitable. Except for natural phenomena such as hurricanes and the like, most events are caused by people. Indeed, it is becoming increasingly evident today that even seemingly natural catastrophes such as floods, earthquakes, droughts, and changes in climate are often induced or exacerbated by human tampering. These observations suggest that by understanding how our activities affect the natural and social environments, by disciplined utopia building, and by careful selection of alternatives of action, we may be able to reduce the probabilities of catastrophe and create a better future for ourselves and our descendants.

But how can we build useful utopias, how can we plan, how can we stave off catastrophe when so few of us agree about what courses of action would be best to follow? Should we just muddle along, each person watching out for his own lawful interests, or can we and should we consciously shape our future?

Free Will and Determinism

Underlying some of the social, economic, and political disagreements that separate people in planning for the future are differing assumptions about the extent to which "free will" and "determinism" shape the unfolding of human affairs.

One tendency is to underscore each person's free will to the point where it seems useless and even dangerous to look for historical patterns and repetitions, to forecast future trends, or to design alternate causes of action. Those who see the problem this way often resist efforts to discover a science of human behavior in that it seems to deny a person's uniqueness as a particular human being. To stuff an individual's yearnings, predispositions, values, and activities into scientific hypotheses or, even worse, into mathematical equations and computer programs is viewed as mechanistic, deterministic, a threat to one's basic humanity. Another tendency is to focus upon inexorable forces of one kind or another, to see human affairs as essentially predetermined by biological laws, instincts, ideology, economics, or social habit. Such an approach seems to lock the individual into trends and outcomes that are seen as inevitable. Where does the truth lie?

Individuals and societies alike are clearly limited by their capabilities. Thus, we may conclude that whatever increases or decreases human capabilities will affect the capacity of a person or a group to influence the course of events. To deny this in effect is to deny the possibility of evolution and change, to see twentieth-century man and Paleolithic man as cast in the same unchanging mold, to condemn man to the level at

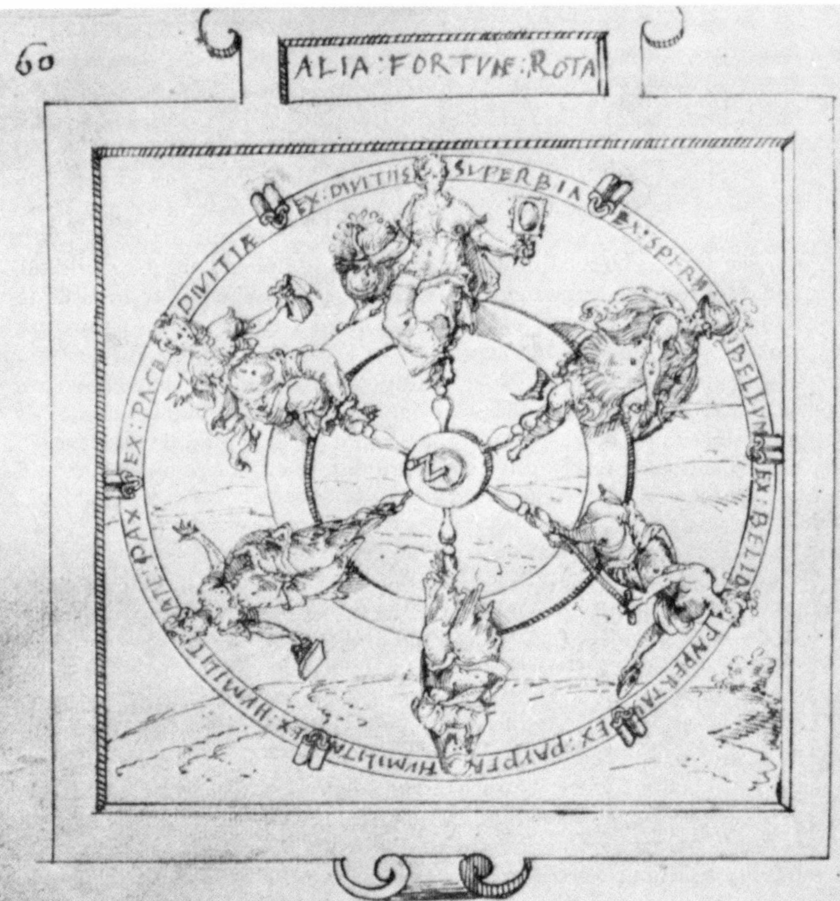

Wheel of Fortune by Jean Cousin.

which he was created. The degree of our slavery to the determination of forces outside (or inside) ourselves and the range of our effective free will are thus relative to our knowledge, skills, and insights at any given time.

A crude analogy may help. For millennia human beings were deterministically terrestrial creatures. No exercise of free will, however heroic, could lift any person more than a few feet from the earth, and efforts to overcome the law of gravity led to disaster, as Icarus and others discovered. Slowly and painfully, however, human beings learned enough about the universal laws of their physical environment to harness natural forces and thrust clear of the determinisms to which they had been enslaved previously. Once they had built a properly constructed spaceship, humans could propel themselves to the moon and back with only a relatively few interventions—an acceleration to get into earthly orbit, an acceleration to free themselves of the earth's gravitational field, and so forth. Natural laws did the rest, and people thus emancipated themselves from the strictures of gravity. Science and engineering had come to understand, intervene in, cooperate with, and harness some of the forces that formerly kept us deterministically imprisoned.

All of us living today confront the current system break with an entirely different set of capabilities than did our ancestors in the revolutions that resulted from the shaping of stone tools, the control of fire, or even the unleashing of steam and electricity. With their limited understanding of natural forces, our earliest forebears could only cooperate with them. Many Stone Age rituals and ceremonies were celebrations of human cooperation with nature's ebbs and flows. And to a large extent, in common with their animal cousins, our early forebears created problems that were readily kept in check and managed by nature's own regulatory arrangements. When a local population grew too large for the resources ultimately available to it, famine trimmed the numbers. But as human technology advanced, arrangements fabricated by people tended to override nature's feedbacks, allowing runaway growth on important dimensions. Unfortunately, in acquiring their new practical sophistications, people tended to put their accumulating knowledge into separate boxes, each with its own categorical, Aristotelian label. Consequently, people have tended to lose their earlier intuitive feel for nature's ebbs and flows and limiting feedbacks.

While our ancestors used religion (what, in retrospect, we often refer to as magic) and complex ritual to explain and cope with the workings of their world, we today rely increasingly on science (which amounts to our own form of magic) to explain the various mysteries of nature.

But not content with mere understanding and self-adjustive coping, we have tried to override nature as the pacesetter for the environment and for ourselves. Particularly since the beginning of the industrial revolution, there has been an upsurge in the human capacity for intervening in natural processes. These interventions in the economy of nature have significantly shifted the balance of influence between the impact of natural forces and the impact of human activities. Paradoxically, it sometimes appears that as we gain control over the forces of nature, we have greater difficulty seeing and understanding the consequences of our actions.

Can we learn soon enough to use our technology wisely, with concern for the future, or must we wait for a major catastrophe before discovering our true role in nature and devising less destructive, more stable, and more humane ways of living and working with one another? The answer depends upon what kind of creatures we are and what our potentials for further development may be. Unfortunately, it may be much more difficult to understand and improve ourselves and our institutions than to acquire knowledge about the purely mechanical aspects of the universe and its workings.

Some Further Constraints on the Human Potential

Human ideas, dispositions, and behavior seem to emerge from a variety of sources. Many of our day-to-day activities are shaped by our biological background (our need for food, water, air, and living space) and by our combined cognitive and affective predispositions (our perceptions, our ability to project into the future, our ability to find release for our feelings in a variety of ways). But there are apparent flaws and limitations in these capacities. As a psychologist friend once put it, human beings are not "wired very well" for survival in a nuclear age. For example, some of the more stable patterns of behavior are those associated with people's acquisitiveness, aggressiveness, and common reactions to perceived injury or threat. These dispositions may have helped us to survive and to develop our capabilities, but in an age of push-button destruction they are becoming increasingly dangerous.

On the other hand, as we learn more about ourselves (the biological laws to which we are subject and the feelings, thoughts, and activities toward which we are disposed), we may find ways to sharpen our insights, widen our alternatives, free ourselves from the limitations of our past, and open up wholly new possibilities for innovation and fulfillment. Yet a central and highly controversial question remains: how much of a person's self or nature is determined or wired in, and to what extent is this wiring inflexible and unchangeable?

There is a widespread tendency to perceive human nature as more immutable, less variable, less capable of learning than it really is because of our failures to be sufficiently clear about the new environments and relationships that we might aspire to. A little thought and observation should persuade us, however, that the hostile, aggressive, and other potentially destructive feelings that we all experience do not *necessarily* lead to hostile activities. In a favorable environment we are often able to sublimate feelings of anger, frustration, and aggression into constructive, cooperative, and creative behavior. The difficulty is that from the viewpoint of many individuals and often of whole societies, the prevailing social environment is not conducive to such sublimation and creative effort. All too often we demand our individual protections and privileges while insisting on the right to improve our individual positions to the greatest extent possible. And often we try to justify this personal right by presenting ourselves as better born, more skillful, more intelligent, harder working, more virtuous, or otherwise more deserving than our rivals, our neighbors, and even our friends.

Difficulties in Social Learning

During major transitions or system breaks, technological advances seem to race ahead of the human capacity for social learning. Often considerable time elapses between an event and some of its critical results, so that the connection between the two is missed, and a valuable lesson may not be learned. Hence it is difficult to undertake social, economic, and political innovations, however beneficial, with any sense of confidence that they will be accepted by the community or society at large. Already we have the capacity, in our nuclear and other technology, to create outcomes that affect not only our children and grandchildren, but the lives and welfare of people who will not be born for a thousand years or more. But the constructive and destructive consequences of our decisions today—how much to depend on nuclear reactors in obtaining energy, for example—will not be evident for a long time to come. To a considerable extent it is precisely the great amount of time that may elapse between a major social, economic, political, or other action of a society and the possibility of evaluating its consequences which makes social learning a slow and uncertain process. A baby who has touched a hot stove feels the burn immediately, but the harm or benefit of a public policy may not be felt for months, years, or even decades.

Among many social scientists there is a growing consensus that very little is understood about how large and complex social systems, including states and empires, really work. All too often, the intuitively obvious outcome of a policy or action does not occur. And all too often, the program that is undertaken to solve a problem—whether to alleviate highway crowding, fight crime, reduce the number of people on welfare, regenerate a ghetto, deter an enemy, or reduce armaments—has a reverse effect or, in solving one difficulty, creates another.

Social systems are characterized by *multifinality* and *equifinality*; that is, similar paths of behavior often lead to different outcomes, and similar outcomes are often reached by different paths. The structure of a social system, the relationships among the parts, and any persisting trends may therefore be more important than its condition or behavior at any particular moment. Thus the critical significance of a country's population may not be its size at the last census, but its technology, the range and availability of its resources, and the direction and rate of change of each of these three variables.

According to Jay Forrester of MIT, a pioneer in model building, in "Counterintuitive Behavior of Social Systems" (*ZPG National Reporter*, June 1971), most social systems have relatively few influence points through which the behavior of the system can be changed. Often such influence points are not located where the decision makers or analysts expect them to be. Governmental subsidies may not save a private railroad from bankruptcy, for example, or the dispatch of troops to a foreign country may not prevent a communist victory. Furthermore, Forrester explains, if someone has identified a point where influence can be exerted, the chances are still that such a person "guided by intuition and judgment will alter the system in the wrong direction." Thus, rather than reducing traffic jams, the building of a freeway system may encourage more people to drive their cars to work and therefore create larger tie-ups.

Many social systems, according to Forrester, are "inherently insensitive to most policy changes that people select in an effort to alter the behavior of the system. In fact, a social system tends to draw our attention to the very points at which an attempt to intervene will fail. Our experience, which has been developed from contact with simple systems, leads us to look close to the symptoms of trouble for a cause." We may then end up treating the symptom without ever locating the cause. Traditional approaches to poverty, crime, revolution, and war may provide examples: we assume too readily that a welfare program will be sufficient to eradicate poverty; that prison sentences and capital punishment will necessarily reduce crime; that police tactical squads will prevent revolution; or that massive armaments can be relied upon to preclude war. In fact, none of these precautions gets at the roots of the problems that inspire it.

A part of the difficulty is that theoreticians and practitioners alike tend to focus too exclusively on certain aspects of the system at the expense of other aspects. "It is my basic theme," writes Forrester, "that the human mind is not adapted to interpreting how social systems behave. Our social systems belong to the class called multiloop nonlinear feedback systems. In the long history of evolutions it has not been necessary for man to understand these systems until very recent historical times." Today we can no longer afford to remain ignorant of how large, complex social systems work.

By the term *multiloop*, Forrester means in part that when a system such as a nation-state has acted, the awareness of the impact of this action on the part of those who made that decision is achieved through a number of different, perhaps quite complicated channels of communication. Each time a president of the United States escalated the war in Vietnam, reports of various consequences, many of them contradictory in their import, were "fed back" to decision makers in Washington as well as to the public at large. Often the views of the war that were formed in this way turned out in the long run to be so confusing that a wide range of different policy conclusions might be drawn from them and subsequently acted upon.

Forrester's use of the term *nonlinear* refers to the common tendency of social systems to respond to some event in the environment not arithmetically, merely adding one increment of activity to another, but geometrically, multiplying by the square or cube perhaps. It is well known that populations tend to increase exponentially, but we are less likely to be aware of the tendency for people to respond geometrically or exponentially to perceptions of threat or emotionally arousing stimuli. International crises frequently come about when Country *A* makes a threatening move toward Country *B*, who responds with a larger counterthreat, which stimulates *A* to undertake a still larger counter-counterthreat, and thus the conflict spirals or "explodes." Since each move by each of the parties was intended to deter the other party from some activity, the tit-for-tat interchange is likely to produce an outcome that is almost precisely the opposite of what *A* and *B* actually wanted.

Having observed the frequency with which such processes have taken place in human history, Forrester concludes that we tend to learn the wrong lessons from such experiences, falling back on the same habitual responses over and over again. Thus, he contends, evolutionary processes have failed to provide us with the mental skills needed to properly interpret the dynamic behavior of the complex systems we have created and of which we have become a part. As a consequence, a society "may suffer a growing sense of futility" as it repeatedly attacks the same old deficiencies while the "systems continue to worsen."

Human Interactivity

While trying to deal with worldwide problems involving millions, even billions, of people, we confront at the same time a fundamental need on the part of individual human beings for a sense of integrity and possibilities for self-expression and growth. Often such individual aspirations are challenged as a threat to the collective good. Yet no collectivity can exist apart from what its individual members are willing to put up with and contribute. Viewed altogether, these considerations present something of a paradox: can the well-being of a whole society be achieved without limiting the possibilities of individual self-fulfillment? Conversely, can a society achieve satisfactory outcomes as long as considerable numbers of individual members are frustrated and suffering from a feeling of alienation?

To a large extent individuals and small groups are deeply influenced by the societies of which they are a part. This social sensitivity seems to be characteristic of those within a society who oppose it as well as its more conforming members. But the loyalists and the opposition may draw contradictory conclusions from their day-to-day experiences, the former feeling rewarded by what the society offers and more inclined to sublimate their destructive impulses, the latter growing progressively more alienated, aggressive, and perhaps violent. Initially, the number of dissidents in a society may be small, but if over a period of time the relatively agreeable circumstances of more and more of the loyalists worsen, some are likely to join the opposition. If large numbers turn to dissidence, a revolution may take place. For the feelings, thoughts, and habits of the revolutionary (and of the drug addict, alcoholic, indigent, and criminal as well) are partly the result of their interactions not only with family members and other individuals, but also with larger groups, the community, and the society as a whole.

Because of widely shared, deep-seated values and habit structures, however, even a revolution that overthrows a long-established government and alters some social, economic, and political institutions in obvious ways may not, in the long run, make as much difference in people's lives as we might expect. Often such a revolution does little more than substitute a new ruling elite for the old. From a broader perspective, the amount of actual social learning resulting from such a revolution may be quite minimal. Thus, the French Revolution, which expressed liberty, equality, and fraternity, opened the way for the Napoleonic Empire. And under Stalin, the Bolshevik revolution was transformed into the powerful dictatorship of a few. In general, therefore, we

"You have the floor: explain yourself; you're free" by Honoré Daumier.

may expect beliefs, values, expectations, institutions, and behavior to persist over considerable periods of time—especially when the benefits of a revolution are unequally distributed or differentially apparent to members of the society at large. When the rare, monumental system breaks do occur—the agricultural revolution of the Neolithic Age, for example, or the industrial revolution of more recent times—they often stem from revolutions of technology that disrupt societies worldwide from the bottom up and leave everyone living in notably different ways.

There are parallels on international levels where conflicts, crises, and wars may result from the policies and actions of individual countries with divergent capabilities and interests whose behavior appears entirely legitimate to their own citizens and leaders. Since World War II, for example, conflicting goals and activities of Arabs and Israelis in the Middle East have appeared eminently reasonable from their respective viewpoints, even though the outcomes of their *interactions* have been destructive to both sides and dangerously threatening to world peace.

Problems of Level and Hierarchy

It is tempting to explain the behavior of communities, commercial and industrial firms, nation-states, and other large and complex social systems primarily in terms of the interests, dispositions, and decisions of top leaders. But the patterns and effects of human interaction operate vertically—between social, economic, and political levels within a society—as well as horizontally, across societies. A large amount of routine, though often extremely influential, decision making takes place in the bureaucracies of government and private industry. Departments and department heads, divisions and division chiefs, to say nothing of higher officers, often pursue immediate goals that have very little to do with national goals and policies. A low-level clerk knows that his influence will be increased and his salary improved if he can supervise an assistant or two. Departments compete for funds and influence. A young Pentagon colonel hopes that by recommending a new weapons system he may be able to make brigadier general, just as a young engineer in a defense firm sees possibilities for a major research and development project which, if funded, would greatly advance his career. The colonel and the engineer, if they collaborate successfully, may develop a whole new industry producing weapons which require, in turn, a matching military doctrine, and, over time, a growing proportion of the country's military budget.

Many powerful trends and drifts are generated on still lower levels by people like you and me. Our simplest demands, if shared by millions of other people, can contribute in major ways to the sociology, economics, and politics of the society as a whole. Over the last three generations, living patterns in the United States have changed enormously as more and more Americans bought one and then two cars per family; as they watched motion pictures, purchased radios and, later, television sets; as they gave up trains for planes; as women and girls took birth control pills; and so forth. These changes in living patterns contributed in obvious ways to changes in the values, aspirations, expectations, and further activities of American society.

There are other changes that have not always been so obvious. Five mornings a week millions of us start up our smog-generating machines and drive to work. We all contribute to the pollution of the atmosphere, but the amount of each person's contribution is so small that no one of us is likely to be much disturbed by the contamination for which he or she is personally responsible. It is the yellow, eye-smarting haze created by "all those other people" that disturbs us. Indeed, the pollution generated by each of us is so relatively unimportant, especially when measured against the clear importance of our undertakings, that most of us see no reason for cutting back, at least not until everyone else does. Thus it is brought about, through a kind of social determinism, that day in and day out the air will be polluted.

The consequences of small decisions and actions undertaken by you, me, and millions of others may extend far beyond our national borders. Today we know that if several million Americans consume an additional gallon of gasoline a day, or drink one more cup of coffee for breakfast each morning, or use more sugar in their cooking, the relationship between this country and nations in South America, Africa, or the Middle East may be affected in important ways. Vast numbers of individual decisions in other countries—especially other large, industrialized countries—have comparable effects in the world.

In his concept of the "tragedy of the commons," Garrett Hardin has tried to capture a related difficulty. Every human being on earth, writes Hardin, "constitutes a draft on all aspects of the environment: food, air, water, forests, beaches, wildlife, scenery, and solitude." In a system of private property, people who enjoy the ownership of property recognize their responsibility to care for it, for if they did not, they would eventually suffer. "A farmer, for instance, will allow no more cattle in a pasture than its carrying capacity justifies. If he overloads it, erosion sets in, weeds take over, and he loses the use of the pasture."

On the other hand, if this same pasture becomes a commons open to all, the right of each to use it may not be matched by a corresponding responsibility to protect it. Obviously if each user of the commons were to exercise constraint, there would be no problem, but it takes only one person to destroy such a system of voluntary restraint. "Asking everyone to use it with discretion will hardly do," Hardin continues, "for the considerate herdsman who refrains from overloading the commons suffers more than a selfish one who says his needs are greater."

But in today's crowded world of human beings who are less than perfect, "mutual ruin is inevitable if there are no controls." Hardin believes that the air and the water have become polluted because they are treated as commons. And further, the population growth or per capita conversion of natural resources into pollutants will only make the problem worse.

Hardin's metaphor may be somewhat misleading, however. Property owners have been known to exploit their own "pastures," preferring high profits in the short run (when market prices are high, for example) to benefits spread over a longer term. This tendency to get in and out of an enterprise is likely to be especially strong in terms of nonrenewable resources such as oil or coal or even a potentially renewable resource such as timber. Similar to this possibility is the not uncommon disposition to harvest a pasture for one resource, such as oil or land for suburban development, which yields a quick profit, at the expense of another resource, such as its food producing capacity. Conversely, strong motivations for the care and preservation of a commons can emerge from sectors of a society that do not own it. Until comparatively recently, for example, pressures for the conservation of forests, lakes, streams, and coastlines often emerged from sectors of the general public rather than from the people who owned these resources and were determined to exploit them as rapidly as possible.

There is an even more serious difficulty with Hardin's argument in that he attributes what may be a disproportionate part of the wastage of the earth and its resources to "improvidence," as he chooses to define it. In his words, "A wise and competent government saves out of the production of the good years in anticipation of bad years to come. Joseph taught this policy to Pharaoh in Egypt more than 2,000 years ago. Yet the great majority of the governments of the world do not follow such a policy."

Specifically, Hardin appears to confuse economic and technological efficiency, which is presumably high in the industrialized nations and low in the poor nations, with overall efficiencies in terms of long-range human and global outcomes. He seems to imply, for example, that it is the poor, and only the poor, who are improvident and who drain the earth of its resources. Yet, even the *average* person in a highly industrialized country consumes many times the resources used by an average person in a poor country, and rich people in poor and rich countries alike use vastly disproportionate amounts of resources. In today's world, however, providing for the future well-being and stability of human societies may depend not only on saving out of this year's production but also on a narrowing of the wide gaps between the consumption of the rich and the consumption of the poor. It also means developing a year-in and year-out balance between human demands and the long-term capacity of the earth to yield resources.

If consumption of mechanical energy from all major sources—coal, oil, wood, hydroelectrical generation, and so forth—is translated into kilograms of coal equivalents, world consumption per capita in 1975 was calculated at 2,059 kilograms. For the developing countries, per capita consumption was very much lower, 394 kilograms, whereas for the developed countries per capita consumption was 6,349 kilograms. For representative individual countries, the gaps were considerably wider (see *Table 1*).

Table 1: Per Capita Consumption of Primary Energy

Country	*Kilograms of Coal Equivalents*
United States	11,485
Sweden	5,804
USSR	5,252
Japan	3,839
People's Republic of China	650
Burundi	13

Source: *World Energy Supplies*, Series J, No. 19 (New York: United Nations, 1976, Table 2, pp. 10–123).

From these simple data it is evident that the addition of one person to the population of the United States generates almost a thousand times the drain upon global supplies of primary energy as that created by the addition of one Burundian. This observation suggests that population growth is not the only critical consideration. *It is a combination of population growth and rising standards of living that taxes the earth and its resources most heavily.* Thus future world stability may depend upon a moderation in the resource demands of the rich (rich countries as well as rich individuals) in addition to a slowing down of population growth in the poor countries.

The world per capita level of energy consumption of 2,059 kilograms of coal equivalent—if it were evenly available to the population of the earth (and if other critical resources were similarly allocated)—would go a long way toward providing humankind everywhere with such requirements of life as food, housing, health facilities, and other elementary goods and services in sufficient quantities to lower infant mortality, make everyone literate, and increase life expectancy to 70 years or more. Against this background, it is significant that a large proportion of energy consumption in the relatively rich, industrialized nations is accounted for not by their basic needs but by their military establishments, automobiles, appliances, and other comparative luxuries. These observations signify that the situation is not hopeless. On the contrary, *a leveling off of world population growth combined with a moderation in our demands for non-necessities and a more equitable allocation of resources worldwide* might provide an eminently livable habitat for ourselves and our descendants for many generations to come.

Other Difficulties in Approaching the Future

The problem of how to maintain the earth as a favorable habitat is not as simple as the previous pages may seem to suggest. It is relatively easy to call for a tapering off of population growth, moderation in resource consumption, and a more equitable allocation of the world product, but it is a much more difficult task to bring such changes about. In part, this difficulty arises because people who are accustomed to consuming substantially more than the world average are likely to resist any serious consideration of a thoroughgoing redistribution. But there are other more elusive and complex reasons why such massive changes in human affairs are not easily brought about.

Among these is the growth paradox. A certain amount of growth is considered desirable, even necessary, for a vigorous society. Unless a country's production increases year by year, the economy may be depressed and large numbers of people may suffer. Historically, those societies that have ceased to grow economically and technologically have often suffered decline. But unlimited growth over an extended period of time may contribute to resource scarcities, pollution, urban stagnation, trade imbalances, international conflicts on various levels, and outright war.

Strong growth in a country's economy and production capacity may increase competition with other countries for resources, markets, and the strategic advantages considered necessary for securing trade routes. This consideration often leads to a further paradox. In seeking to strengthen its own position, each country tends to validate the competitive anxieties of its rivals. As resources are depleted or markets flooded, each of the countries is likely to redouble its efforts, thus exacerbating demands and competitive anxieties.

In recent years this paradox has assumed new and complicated dimensions. Until World War I, and to a lesser extent thereafter, the industrialized countries of the world were able to secure protected access to resources and markets through colonial expansion. This is no longer the case today. Although the world is still characterized by powerful industrialized countries, new sovereignties in Asia, Africa, and elsewhere have replaced the former colonies, and physical possession of colonial territory is no longer feasible. Penetration of these developing countries has accordingly become both more complex (requiring modern techniques, institutions, and organizations for the conduct of foreign affairs) and more crucial, with the realization, by strong and weak societies alike, of the need for secure access to energy and other resources in a world of scarcities.

During recent decades, rival powers have developed ingenious new mechanisms for pursuing their interests in foreign countries, all of which can be viewed as manifestations of expansionism. This is true whether we are concerned with Soviet assistance to the People's Republic of China during the 1950s and to Middle Eastern, African, Latin American, and Southeast Asian countries; or with American or Western European economic, technical, and military aid and Peace Corps operations throughout much of the Third World. The situation has been made even more complex by the development of multinational corporations. Extending their activities across national boundaries, these huge firms are often able to increase their individual effectiveness by taking advantage of favorable conditions in a number of different societies—cheap labor, abundant raw materials, readily available capital, favorable tax rates, and so forth. Many economies are undoubtedly achieved in this way, and multinational corporations commonly emphasize their capacity for making technology, capital, and a certain amount of employment available to developing societies. Such organizations are also accused, however, of benefiting only a limited number of elite specialists in developing societies, and the governments at home and host governments alike may find them difficult to regulate. In the long run, the activities of multinational corporations in their present form may exacerbate the tragedy of the commons.

For individuals, and for societies even more, there may be serious incompatibilities between short-term and long-term interests. All too frequently, national leaders are inclined to favor decisions that yield early benefits, despite awareness that the longer-range costs may be extremely high. In discounting the future this way, high-level decision makers may well be responding to pressures from the rest of us who would rather enjoy an assured advantage today than to invest in tomorrow's uncertainties. As noted by engineer Harold Linstone in "Planning: Toy or Tool" (*IEEE Spectrum*, April 1974), "The forecaster points to distant threats and opportunities only to find a frustrating and maddening unresponsiveness. He is a victim of the law: short-term problems drive out long-range planning." Most of us tend to shrug off the more distant future. In the long run we are all dead anyway, or *après moi, le déluge*.

The situation is complicated further by the fact that in any hierarchy of systems there is likely to be a conflict between the goals of a subsystem and the interests of the broader system. Higher taxes unbalance my budget but provide better schools for my neighbor's children. A large and sudden influx of skilled workers into a small town may be good for the new firm that has established itself there but not for the community as a whole. And on an international level the foreign policies of individual countries normally emphasize the security and well-being of each particular society but seldom take the welfare of neighboring states or the world at large into adequate account.

In the past many of the problems, inconsistencies, paradoxes, and conflicts inherent in large and complex social systems have been inadequately understood. Law-abiding citizens fail to perceive how they may be fostering the environments for crime. Entrepreneurs and policymakers remain blind to the longer-term costs of today's decisions. Conservationists are slow to understand how the measures they propose may affect employment and the economy at large. It scarcely occurs to many patriotic citizens how a strategic, economic, or political gain for their country may damage or perhaps annihilate innocent people in another country. Frequently the incompatibilities, competitions, conflicts, confrontations, and crises emerging from inconsistencies and paradoxes that are built into the system have been treated only as moral or legal issues, each individual adversary or interest group attributing evil intent to the opponent. The effects of the structure of the encompassing social system may thus be overlooked. As Linstone notes, "Rational microdecisions all too frequently lead to irrational macrodecisions," and seemingly rational macrodecisions constrain and contradict what appear to be rational microdecisions.

Today, with the many societies of the world living almost elbow-to-elbow with each other and with virtually instant communications, faster-than-sound transportation, resource scarcities, widespread pollution, and potential mass destruction at the push of a button, we can no longer allow these built-in conflicts merely to take care of themselves. A first step is to recognize that many of these incompatibilities are not necessarily the perpetration of evil people, but are often inherent in large, highly stratified, intensely competitive social structures. A second step is to devise new institutions—or to resurrect old ones—which can regulate and reduce some of these conflicts and discrepancies in ways that are understandable, relatively noncoercive, and optimally just.

Equality by Jean-François Millet.

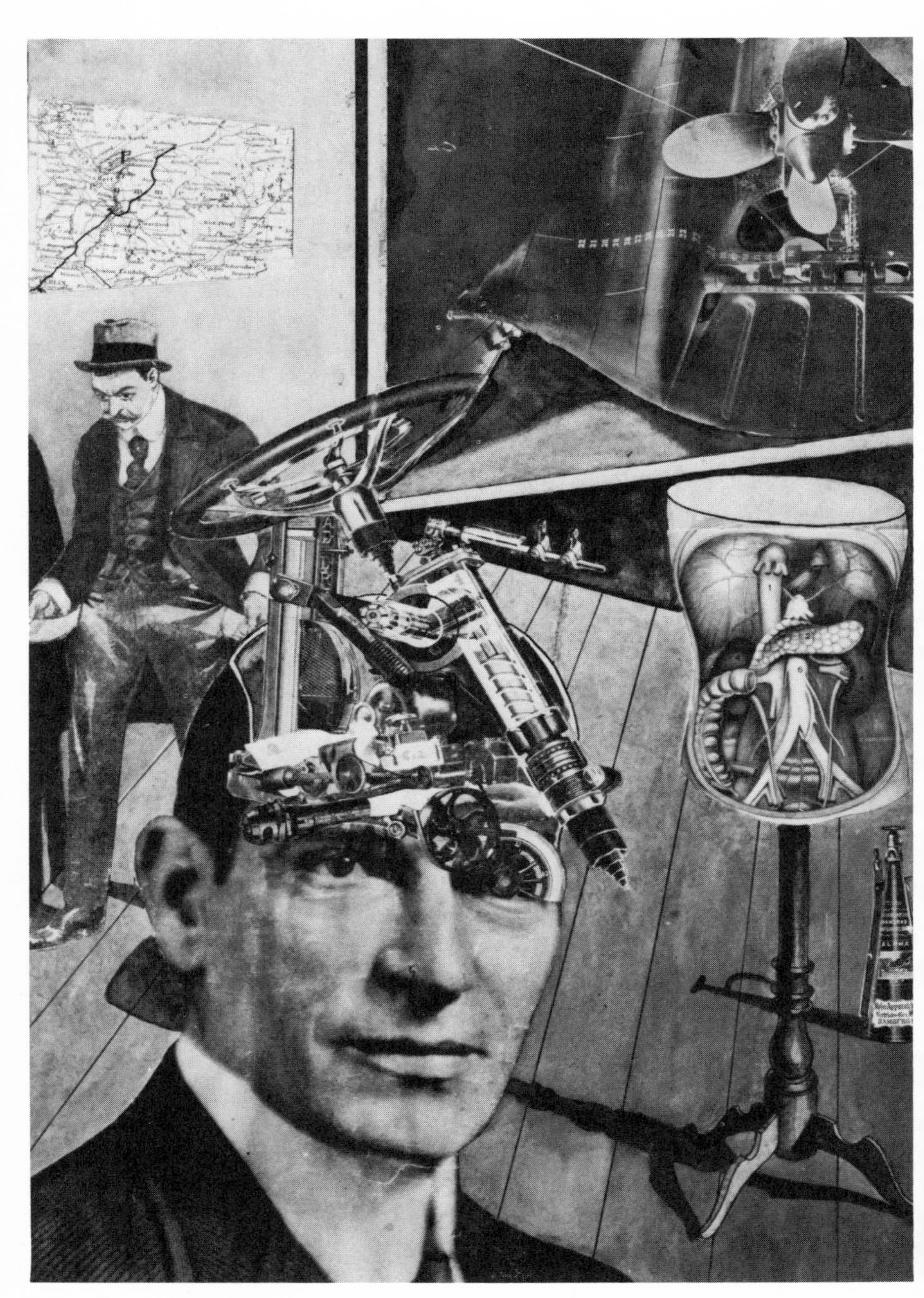

Tatlin at Home by Raoul Hausmann.

CHAPTER SIX

THE UNDERLYING DYNAMICS OF SOCIAL SYSTEMS

IN EARLIER CHAPTERS I have referred to human motivation as a product of each person's previous interactions with the physical environment, other individuals, different organizations, and society as a whole. In simplest terms we can thus envisage a person's activities in part as a continuing effort to cope with events in his or her environment. Since both the physical and social environments are continually changing, a person is never entirely at rest but is always responding to one degree or another in feeling, thought, and behavior. We know that people often respond quite differently to the same or similar events and conditions. It is also evident that people have the ability to project hypothetical events and conditions into the future and to pursue them as goals. These relationships are further complicated by the fact that, in responding to events and in pursuing goals, people alter the physical and social environments that are affecting them. In this way we are continually influencing our own futures.

Among our many goals, most of us aspire generally to a good life, or at least a life that is an improvement over what we have become accustomed to. There are, of course, a great many different factors that can affect our concepts and definitions of the "good life," and the way we feel about them will depend a great deal upon where and under what conditions we live, how we were brought up, what we expect and aspire to, and so forth. We cannot give much serious attention to problems of the future without taking such factors into account.

In his book *Motivation and Personality*, psychologist Abraham Maslow has conceived of human needs and aspirations as a pyramid-shaped hierarchy arising from 1) a base of physiological needs including food, water, air, and so forth; to 2) safety needs such as a reasonably stable environment, protection, and a sense of personal security; 3) belonging and love needs involving membership in a group, affection, and the like; 4) esteem needs including a sense of freedom, achievement, attention, importance, and dignity; and 5) the need for self-actualization, which refers to the human desire for self-fulfillment, for becoming what one potentially is. As the "lower," more basic physiological needs are satisfied to some extent, the next level of hierarchy—the safety needs—becomes salient, and so forth on toward self-actualization at the top.

Among the weaknesses of the Maslow model is the possibility that it will be viewed too narrowly—almost like a ladder to success—and interpreted to mean that self-actualization is best achieved through the satisfaction, first, of physical needs and yearnings for belonging and achievement, followed only later by a sense of self-fulfillment. But do we have sound reasons for concluding that the Paleolithic hunter or toolmaker, the Neolithic potter, the tribal chief, or the shaman had less possibility for self-actualization than the modern artist with rich patronage, the prize-winning physicist, the television evangelist, or the board chairman of a multinational corporation? Probably the better way to view the Maslowian hierarchy is according to an interactive arrangement wherein all the various needs are related to one another in a person's undertakings and managed in reciprocally supportive ways. We might also infer that comparative values may be more important than absolute ones. That is, the ghetto-dweller with a secondhand Cadillac may feel deprived compared with his neighbors in an affluent housing development across the freeway, whereas the Paleolithic toolmaker may have rested secure in the knowledge that he would receive his equal share of the next successful hunt.

Thus, self-fulfillment may mean quite different things to any number of people, but to the extent that Maslow is correct in putting physical needs at the base of his pyramid, we may conclude that a society's allocation of resources is likely to affect the middle and higher levels in important ways. A few strong-willed or especially talented ghetto dwellers may achieve self-actualization, of course, just as numbers of affluent people may live in torment. Overall, however, self-actualization may be more attainable by those who have lived in societies where both physical and psychic resources are more or less equally available to all, rather than by those who find themselves in any extreme position of either wealth or poverty, within an inequitable environment. In any case, we would expect linkages between relative access to resources and opportunities for esteem and self-actualization to be critical for whole societies in dealing with one another as well as for individuals and groups within a single society. As on the individual level, self-actualization may be difficult to achieve in societies that, compared with others, are either very poor or very rich—especially if the allocation of resources in either case is grossly inequitable.

Interrelationships Between Quantity and Quality

Much of the emphasis in this book has been upon the quantitative aspects of our lives—numbers of people, amounts of available resources, technological capabilities, and so forth. We may thus appear to have neglected the qualities of life as suggested in Maslow's pyramid—fellowship, love, affection, freedom, esteem, achievement, and self-fulfillment. But this emphasis has been deliberate, being part of an effort to focus upon the inseparable relationships that exist between the quantity of things and the quality of things that people deal with. Often, the tendency is quite the opposite: to draw a sharp dichotomy between quantities and qualities, between numbers and values, and to treat them quite separately, as if they were not connected.

A change in the quality of anything almost always involves a change in quantity (dimension, duration, intensity, content, number or proportion of components, and so forth), and, conversely, a change in quantity involves some change in quality. For instance, the quality of steel depends upon numbers—the absolute amounts and proportions of elements employed, the levels and duration of heat applied, and so forth. It may be less evident that the quality of a sculpture or an oil painting depends also upon quantities—the dimensions, proportions, and intensities. So, too, the evaluations of music and poetry change with alterations in the numbers involved—frequencies, intervals, cadences, pitch, intensity, and the like.

The same sort of assertion can be made about quality and quantity in human living: the quality of life is inextricably intertwined with quantities. This generalization applies even to those of us who do not aspire to power or riches. Along with the amount of talent involved, the establishment and maintenance of a symphony orchestra, ballet troupe, art gallery, championship baseball team, children's hospital, or religious retreat depends upon the allocation of time, resources, and human effort. And the potentials of the various physical, social, and cultural resources available within a society will depend upon the size of the

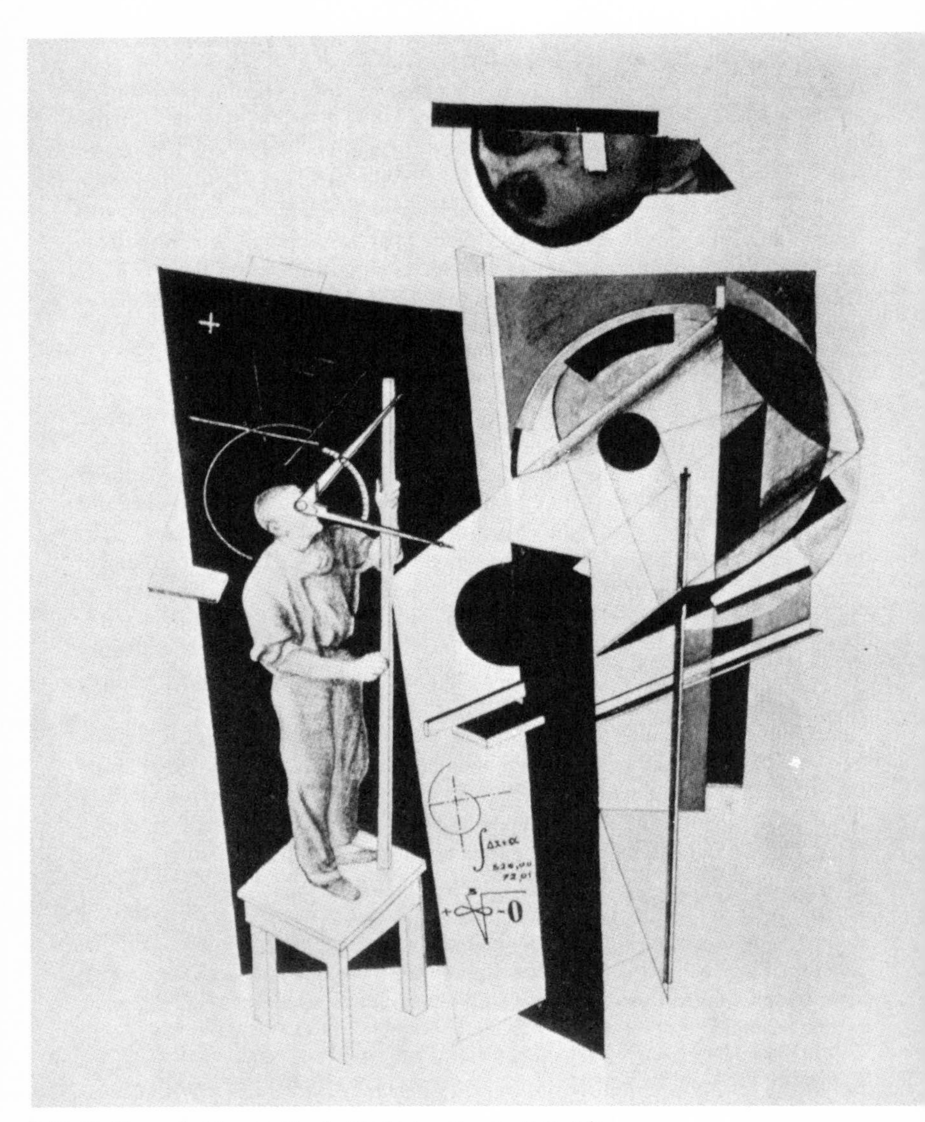

Tatlin Working on the Monument for the Third International by El Lissitzky.

population making demands upon those resources, the level and characteristics of the society's technology, and so forth.

The quality of life within a given society will also be strongly affected by the ways in which its resources are allocated—who gets what, why, how much, and by what means. It is true, of course, that individuals, communities, and whole societies often differ considerably with respect to what they value, but, however great such differences may be, the discrimination of values implies different amounts or proportions of things, including 1) who should gain what benefits, 2) who should pay what costs, and 3) why. These values govern politics and economics in critical ways and constitute some of the moral underpinnings of any community. But the fundamental values of an overall society as described by the answers to these three questions are likely to be altered as population, technology, and access to various types of resources change as well as when the rules for the allocations are changed.

Population-Technology-Resource Variables

We can divide social environments into four categories, each of which is shaped in important ways by the density of its population, the general level of technology, and the resources that are available to the people living in it. As used here, income level serves as a rough indicator of the level of technology and the amount of resources available to a neighborhood, a community, or a larger society:

1. Dense population—High income
2. Dense population—Low income
3. Sparse population—High income
4. Sparse population—Low income

The first environmental category is characteristic of urban and suburban residential areas where people of relative affluence live in apartment houses, condominiums, or high-value family residences in fairly dense but socially exclusive tracts. The second environmental category includes so-called slum or ghetto areas in cities or near the outskirts of cities. The third category refers primarily to rural areas where large, highly productive farms, ranches, recreational facilities, and other enterprises are located and also to suburban areas characterized by private estates or high-cost residential developments. The fourth category applies to low-income rural areas.

A population increase will make a difference in any of the four categories, but the implications will vary from one environmental category to the next: perhaps higher buildings, higher property values, higher rents, and higher incomes as more people crowd into the first; more poverty and crime in the second; the urbanization and commercialization of the third; and severe environmental damage and the creation of larger poverty enclaves in the fourth. Changes in the level of technology and general access to resources will also have parallel but differential effects in the four environments.

We may assume with some confidence that the values, goals, motivations, and behaviors that prevail—and are viewed as norms—within any one of these environments will differ in important ways from those that characterize the other environments. It is also probable that many attitudes and behaviors that are tolerated, if not approved, in one of the four environments will be frowned upon or vigorously condemned in another. In any case, people born and brought up in any one of these environments are likely to have experienced quite different problems from those who are native to one of the other environments. These past experiences will influence a person's attitudes and behaviors throughout a lifetime. And any substantial change in the numbers of people, the level of technology, or the availability of resources in an environment may thus be expected to alter people's values and behavior. Whether we are aware of it or not, such changes—in terms of their outcomes—thus amount to moral choices. Put another way, we can espouse whatever moral platform or school of psychology we wish, but unless these environmental factors are taken into careful account, our explanation or diagnosis of a person's attitudes and behavior will be partial at best.

With respect to each of these environmental sectors we would expect a considerable amount of social behavior to be biased in fairly specific ways. For example, the two high-income environments are likely to be characterized by high per capita consumption in terms of both goods and services, whereas per capita consumption would be much lower in the two low-income environments. But we would also expect the four environments to differ markedly in life-styles, the types of goods and services consumed, psychic and somatic diseases contracted, the crimes committed, and the types of social deviations practiced.

Dense population-high income areas might thus be characterized by high levels of education, opportunities for foreign travel, expenditures for books, music, theater, antiques, and art objects. We might also expect a high incidence of heart attacks and psychiatric disorders arising from intense competition, guilt feelings, boredom, and so forth. Embezzlement might be a characteristic crime. Social relations would probably include fairly high rates of divorce and a certain amount of discreet sexual adventurism. Areas of sparse population and high in-

City Activities by Thomas Hart Benton.

come might involve higher expenditures for horses, private planes and airstrips, private swimming pools, and farm machinery; fractures and hunting accidents; hiring of "wetback" labor; and so forth.

We would expect to find urban ghettos, tenant farming communities, migrant labor camps, and Indian reservations each identifiable by its characteristic responses to the respective environmental settings. In both urban and rural settings low incomes and, in certain environments, utter poverty are almost certain to condition a person's values, expectations, and day-to-day activities in particular but individually distinctive ways. A few people may escape from the environment or find a constructive way to survive in it. Some may give up and live out their lives on welfare. Others may turn to crime. Still others may seek refuge in alcohol or drugs. Despite such differences of individual response, however, environments in which there are severe deprivations, either absolute or comparative, can be expected to produce many undesirable outcomes. If we set out to design and construct a school for crime and other destructive enterprises on the mass level, it would be difficult to produce a more effective setting than a ghetto in a large, modern city—to say nothing of a prison supposedly maintained for "correctional" purposes.

Overall patterns will be complicated further by close juxtapositions of any two or more of the four types of social environments. Thus, a dense population-high income area and a dense population-low income area that are adjoining may affect each other in important ways. Income property in ghettos, for example, is often owned by people who live in high-income environments but who drain off whatever capital is generated in the poverty neighborhood. Ghetto frustrations and hostilities may thus contribute to burglaries and other crimes in affluent neighborhoods. Similarly, a high-density area may create serious pollution in an adjoining area of low density, and the development of a high-income suburb may raise land values in an adjacent rural area to the point where farming is no longer economically feasible.

In this regard it is important to note that heavy transfers of capital from a high-income environment into a low-income environment may create more problems than they solve. Thus the construction of middle- or high-income housing in a former ghetto frequently moves the well-to-do people in and the poverty stricken out in search of some other place to stay. Similarly, welfare regulations may deny to the recipient the possibility of going to school and improving his or her chances of making a living—or of taking a part-time job as a step toward something better. Expensive crime-prevention and rehabilitation programs cannot be expected to succeed unless the criminal can learn a useful trade or profession and obtain a stable job. Future planning that does

Gas by Edward Hopper. 1940.

not get at the source of the problem is at best tinkering with society and at worst is disrupting, threatening, perhaps even destroying it.

There is no single answer to many of the critical problems that confront us. Most of these problems have a variety of causes, and some of the most serious ones appear to begin with the ways in which societies are structured: how basic resources are allocated, who reaps the benefits and who pays the costs of a given enterprise, and so forth. What may be needed, among other innovations, is the development of new balancing mechanisms—new institutions and processes designed to keep societies in better domestic and external equilibrium. Like the inverse feedback mechanisms that the movie Edison needed but did not have, these institutions would use some of the surplus output of more effective enterprises or environments to improve the productivity of less effective enterprises or environments. These capital transfers would not be handouts, however, but would serve as sustained investments in the weaker enterprises.

Transfers of capital (and possibly goods and services) to low-income areas would not be limited to small businesses established by a few enterprising individuals, but would be invested in whatever type and size of undertaking appeared to be rational for the particular environment. Initial costs would almost certainly include the education and training of local people to run the enterprise at all levels, including top management. Residential, health, educational, and other supporting developments would then be associated with the production enterprises and would benefit the community and society at large.

Efforts in such directions have already been made in some ghetto areas and rural poverty enclaves by people organizing themselves for self-improvement. Sporadic attempts have also been made by federal, state, and local governmental agencies. But such efforts will not have persistent or transforming effects unless whole societies are organized along these or comparable lines.

Interrelationships between quality and quantity—and the moral choices involving both—are critical at all levels from the family and community to the society and world at large. And, ultimately, human well-being at each of these levels is related to the possibilities for well-being at other levels. The fundamental problem is how to build these balancing mechanisms into societies in ways that will be flexible, largely self-regulating, and as efficiently, equitably, and democratically administered as possible. But to accomplish these goals over the long run, a society will have to be critically concerned with 1) its population size, 2) its technological trends, 3) its access to resources, and 4) the ways in which these resources are allocated.

Combinations of Population, Technology, and Resources

Suppose that we postulate a society (band, tribe, chiefdom, or state), *A*, which is in a particular condition of balance or equilibrium: it has a population of a given size that is growing at a constant rate; it has access to an adequate amount of resources, and, as the population grows, the flow of accessible resources keeps pace. The society is characterized also by a certain level of technology that advances with the growth of the population and the increasing flow of resources. In other words, the population, resources, and technology stay in more or less fixed proportion: the ratios of each variable to each of the others remains constant through a period of growth and environmental change extending through time.

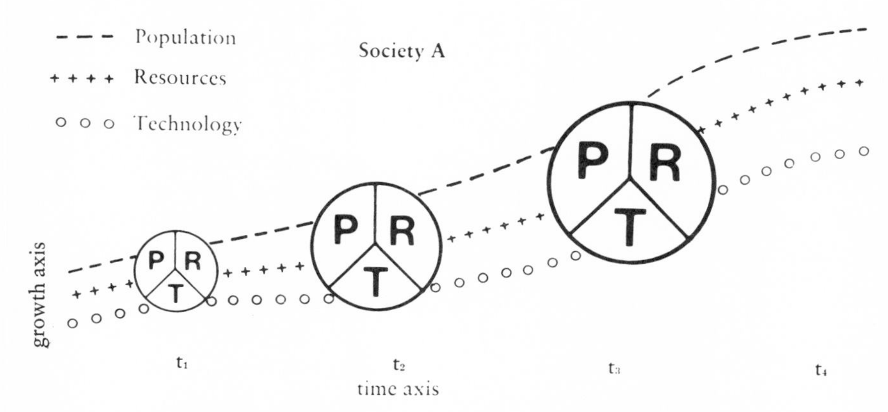

Figure 1: Population, Resources, and Technology in Constant Ratios

Figure 1 depicts a growing society at a given level of organization in some part of the world and during some period of prehistory or history. Characteristically, countries following this pattern have been the major powers which have made heavy demands on resources and have expanded their territory and power in order to obtain them. *Figure 1* might represent the growth of Rome from the union of communities on the Tiber to an Italian republic and then to a vast empire, the growth of France from a small kingdom on the Seine to a powerful European state and a world empire, the growth of England to Great Britain and on to the British Empire with colonies around the world, or the growth of the United States as it expanded from only 13 states along the Atlantic coast to a powerful nation spanning a continent. This figure suggests the progress of each of these societies from inception, through a period of rapid growth to a climax point of maximum growth, wealth, and power. Beyond this point, most powerful societies in history have leveled off in terms of their capabilities and expansionism and have eventually declined. Such declines appear to have been characteristic of many empires in the past: Rome, Britain, France, China (not once, but several times over more than two millennia of history).

During the growth stages, especially in the course of steeper periods of growth following "takeoff," we would expect positive feedbacks to prevail—high rates of population growth and technological advancement, rapid increases in demands and production, and strong tendencies toward the expansion of activities into adjoining territory or overseas colonies. A leveling off of growth processes would indicate a "maturing" of the society with negative feedbacks prevailing; and the period of decline would set in as reverse positive feedbacks began to prevail—previously productive combinations of population, technology, and resources would be disrupted in terms of declining efficiencies and lagging production, perhaps, and/or inadequate access to resources, inflation, unemployment, and the like.

If Society *A*'s balance of population, resources, and technology (PRT) were threatened at t_4 by inadequate access to resources, what prescriptions would be available? The following possibilities come to mind. Society *A* could:

1. Invest more of the national product in technology as a step toward acquiring further resources, keeping in mind that technology creates its own resource demands.
2. Develop the country's military technology and capabilities in order to obtain access to new resources through threat, conquest, or other expansionism.
3. Expand the country's share of trade.
4. Reduce the country's population—a long-term undertaking at best.
5. Discourage population growth while advancing technology in a selective way in order to keep resource consumption as low as possible; develop techniques for obtaining new resources or for using abundant resources in new ways. If this policy were pursued long enough, the society would be able to minimize overall consumption of resources while maintaining per capita consumption at a reasonably high level.

Now let us imagine another society, *B*, which at t_1 is in the same condition of equilibrium as Society *A* was at the same time. But in the case of Society *B*, the population-resource-technology balance—the ratios of each variable to each of the others—does not remain constant. On the contrary, the population variable is allowed to grow at a considerably faster rate than the resource and technology variables.

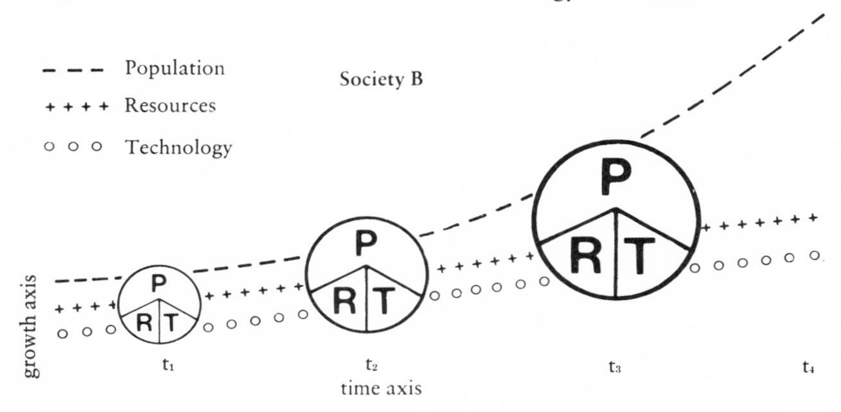

Figure 2: A Society Dominated by High Population Growth

This situation represented by Society *B* suggests what happened in China between about 1650 and the middle of the twentieth century. India has approximated this profile from the seventeenth century to the present. In such instances the population grew faster than the people's ability to acquire resources or to develop appropriate technologies. Indeed, their inability to acquire (as well as transfer and apply) resources resulted, in part, from the lag in the advancement of technology—the failure of these societies to develop ways of obtaining hard-to-get domestic resources or of discovering new uses for old and available resources. The inaccessibility of resources was also a function of the nature of the physical environment and the kinds and arrangement of resources within it.

Since the mid-1950s China, under Maoist policies, has tended to alter this pattern by constraining population growth, advancing basic technologies (especially those combining selected Western techniques with high labor intensity), and acquiring new resources. The People's Republic has increased its access to resources partly by territorial expansion to earlier borders, partly by expropriating and expelling foreign interests, partly by reorganizing the economic and productive relations of society, and partly by applying appropriate techniques to the location, extraction, and processing of domestic resource reserves. To the extent that these trends continue, China might be expected to approximate Society *A* sometime in the future, thus enjoying some of *A*'s benefits and perhaps confronting some of its problems.

A third society, *C*, displays the same condition of equilibrium at t_1. But, in this case, population and technology are allowed to grow more or less commensurately, whereas the access to resources is held relatively constant (see *Figure 3*).

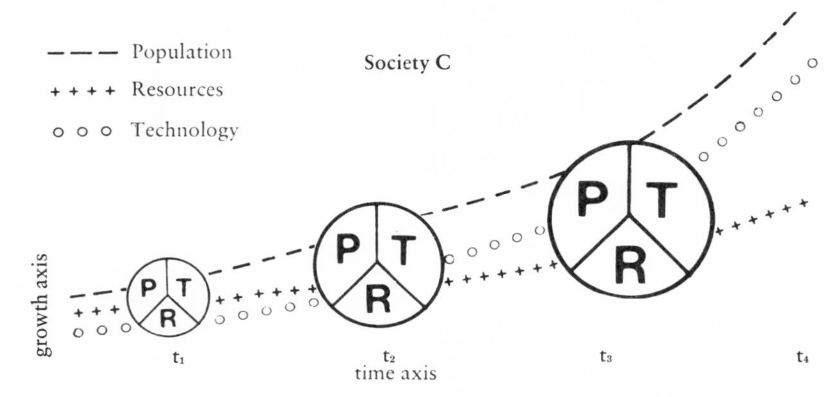

Figure 3: A Growing Society with Inadequate Resources

In the case of Society *C*, since population grows rapidly and technology advances rapidly, we would expect the members of the society to build up their trade capabilities in order to acquire as many resources from the outside as possible. To the extent that trade did not yield sufficient resources, they might also build a powerful military establishment and try to acquire more territory—building either a land or sea empire. In many respects this pattern is like that of Society *A*. The main difference between the two profiles is in the pace of growth and expansion: Society *A* usually requires many generations, perhaps even centuries, to achieve its peak; by contrast, Society *C* may reach its peak in two or three generations in a burst of growth and expansion. The society that comes most readily to mind as an illustration of pattern *C* is Japan between 1870 and 1941.

A society approximating the *C* pattern risks finding itself at the mercy of more powerful countries (*A*-type societies, for example) with greater domestic reserves and/or more powerfully secured access to outside resources. To a considerable extent this was the position that Japanese leaders increasingly perceived their country as occupying relative to

Britain, France, the United States, and even the Netherlands during the 1930s. Aside from developing its military technology and reaching out for resources by threat or conquest, a country approximating Society *C* has very little choice other than 1) to build and maintain an extensive trade network whereby the country is not critically dependent on any particular other country or region for either resources or markets; 2) to develop its technology and train its labor force in order to import raw materials, process them as efficiently as possible, and sell them to foreign markets; and 3) to take what means it can to constrain its population growth and, possibly in the longer run, to reduce its population level.

A quite different life cycle emerges in the case of a fourth society, *D*, which also displays the same condition of equilibrium as the others at t_1. The difference is that Society *D*'s population remains relatively low and stable, whereas its access to resources and its technology increase more rapidly (see *Figure 4*).

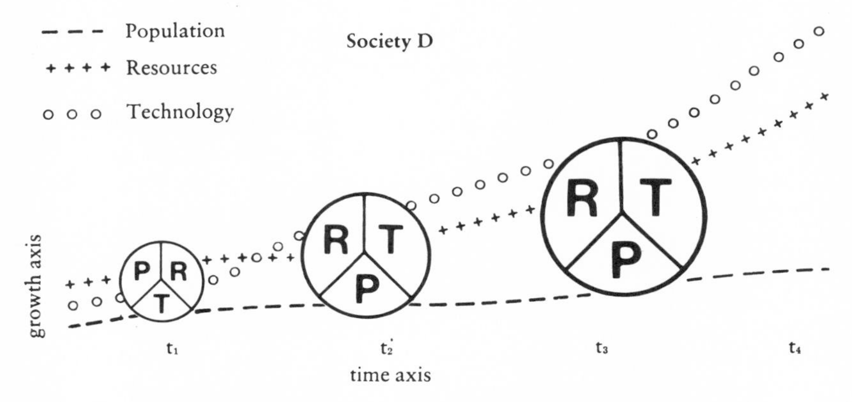

Figure 4: A High Growth-Low Population Society

Society *D* enjoys a steadily increasing per capita share of resources and a per capita increase in the availability of technology. If the people of the society develop their technology wisely, they have the possibility of pursuing optimal quality in their processed goods, rather than mere quantity, and are thus in a position to acquire optimal quality in their material standard of living. Provided they are not attacked from the outside, countries approximating the pattern of Society *D* seem to enjoy optimal political and economic stability. In addition, since their populations are low relative to the level of technology and the availability of resources, per capita access to information, political influence, production, and wealth should be relatively high. The country that seems to approximate this pattern most closely is Sweden during the last century and a half. We can postulate, at least, that if humankind as a whole were to follow the Society *D* pattern—a relatively low world population possessing advanced technologies and access to ample resources—people everywhere might enjoy greater security and generally favorable conditions for self-fulfillment.

Suppose that all the people of the world were governed by a confederation of countries, each of them characterized by a relatively small population, advanced technology, and an abundance of available resources. Individual countries in the confederation would have similar ratios of population, technology and resource availability, but the dimensions themselves might be different. Thus ten million people occupying a relatively unproductive territory might require a larger area in order to have sufficient access to agricultural produce or mineral resources. On the other hand, a commercial or manufacturing society of ten million people might require much less territory provided its access to trade routes and markets could be assured.

The four generalized patterns suggest that throughout prehistory and history the prevailing values, institutions, and behavior patterns of human societies everywhere have been powerfully influenced by the opportunities and resistances presented by the physical and social environments. When the physical environment is harsh, people are more likely to sustain spartan values and habit patterns than they would in more generous surroundings. Similarly, the members of a society may be expected to place a higher value on hard work during earlier stages of their technological advancement compared with later stages, when they can rely upon machines to work for them. So, too, a society flanked by rivals or enemies may live by a somewhat different set of values than one that is relatively isolated or that enjoys good relations with countries it interacts with. We should recognize, however, that a secure society with a small population, a high technology, and relatively abundant resources may suffer disabilities of its own. Sweden, for example, has a worldwide reputation for democratic values, concern for the well-being of its people, and dedication to the idea of peaceful relations with other states. Yet Sweden has suffered some of the malaises, such as high incidences of alcoholism, suicide, and mental illness, that are often assumed to characterize a secure society.

A More Livable Future

Between societies—as well as within societies—a well-ordered, reasonably livable future for us all may well depend upon carefully designed, worldwide inverse feedback arrangements linking the many components of the international system. Such arrangements should enable each country to achieve and maintain viable population-resource-technology balances. In the intermediate to long-run future, the achievement of such worldwide self-regulating mechanisms—like those on neighborhood, community, urban, and domestic regional levels—will require capital flows and ample, immediately available opportunities for hitherto uneducated, unskilled people in vast numbers to achieve *quickly* the knowledge and skills they must have in order to organize, manage, and sustain productive enterprises.

By themselves, these inverse-feedback or balancing arrangements are not likely to be sufficient to create a world society that would be stable, peaceful, and tolerably just, but they may provide a necessary foundation for these further developments. Given such a foundation, people will still confront the problem of how to deal with each other more equitably and how to safeguard the society against perversion or usurpation by interests seeking to aggrandize. The next chapter will discuss some of these problems and consider the possibility that human beings may be able to achieve new levels of comprehension and moral insight enabling us to find solutions. In view of these considerations, a major requirement for smooth transition from the past and the present into the future must involve a better understanding of the linkages and feedbacks that govern relationships between the parts of a society in change as well as between that society and its neighbors.

Still from *Things to Come* by Laszlo Moholy–Nagy.

CHAPTER SEVEN

THE DESIGN OF ALTERNATE FUTURES

IF INDEED THE WORLD is caught up in a major system break comparable to the four great revolutions of the past, then we can expect traditional values and institutions to be subject to massive strains. Many people believe that population increases, unprecedented technological change, and rapid though unevenly distributed economic growth are already threatening traditional values and institutions throughout the world. The implications of these changes are quite different in developing countries than in industrialized countries, but no part of the planet seems likely to escape the revolution that appears to be taking place.

In recent years most of the major problems confronting the United States have become plain to all of us. Inflation erodes the buying power of the wage and salary earner, and, except for those who can find loopholes, taxes spiral unmercifully. The costs of medical, legal, and other vital services rise beyond the reach of millions of people. Decaying cities provide spawning grounds for vicious crime. Courts are overloaded. Public and private bureaucracies often consume talent and resources, but fail to yield commensurate human benefits. Family relationships are increasingly disrupted, the young suffering alienation, the elderly a sense of exile.

To many people in and out of government some of our basic social, economic, and political systems appear to be out of control. In many cases, bureaucracies and top management elites—in both private and governmental sectors—have grown so large and so complex that they elude public accountability. Combining vast power with unbounded secrecy, elements within the FBI and the CIA—with respect to some of their more concealed enterprises—appear to have evaded the scrutiny of Congress, the President, and possibly their own directors as well. In attempting to subvert basic democratic safeguards and processes, the Watergate conspirators, like characters in a shabby melodrama, usurped so much power that they themselves were destroyed by it. Similar problems confound the private sector, where huge chain enterprises squeeze out the independent entrepreneurs, responsible ownership is often dispersed beyond public identification, and multinational corporations evade regulation—thus frustrating the disciplines of legitimate competition.

Many developing countries are threatened by similar problems of inflation, unemployment, bureaucratic inefficiencies, environmental pollution, and costly military development. Often such countries are also beset by war, poverty, famine, and despair. Despite special governmental projects and foreign aid programs, conditions in a number of these societies seem to be getting worse rather than better. Precarious as it already is, the safety of the world will be even more dangerously threatened as unstable governments in some of these societies obtain nuclear weapons.

In poor and rich countries alike the implications of modern warfare defy all logic—not only because of the potential for mass destruction, but also because huge contemporary military establishments are often useless for many purposes of defense and coercion yet absorb large proportions of each year's budgetary allocations and tax burdens. Despite all this, no one seems to know how to stop preparing for war.

Problems of organized human violence—from the political hijacker and the guerrilla unit to large armies and massive nuclear establishments—pose threats to humankind that are unparalleled in the world's history. As the technology of explosives and other weaponry continues to advance, the possibilities of effective control (from control of terrorists to control of proliferating nuclear powers) become increasingly elusive. The greatest minds on earth are hard put to design any kind of fail-safe system that can be counted on to last forever.

For the time being the United States and many other societies can probably survive these threats. Currently, the discrete events that disclose such trends arouse the moral indignation of most of us, although some people persist in rationalizing or even justifying certain of them. It is more difficult to assess what is happening in terms of decay or po-

Galileo surprised at the surface of the earth by Honoré Daumier.

tential collapse of our institutions or systems themselves. For reasons that are not wholly clear, many of us would rather condemn potentially destructive human behavior as the perpetration of evil, conspiratorial forces than as the natural outcome of our own social structures, petty irrationalities, or outright stupidities. To the extent that any considerable number of these trends persist, however, and become unmistakably painful, we may expect increasing numbers of people in this country and in other countries of the world to demand new visions, new alternatives, new ways of doing things.

The critical question then becomes: will these demands give rise to violent revolution? Must human beings suffer catastrophe in order to innovate? Or can we work out, and win acceptance of, new ways of solving our problems not through destruction, chaos, and violence but through massive social learning? The answer is not yet clear.

In addition to these problems, further difficulties arise from the size, complexities, and tendencies for rapid change that characterize many contemporary societies. Over recent generations most industrialized societies and, indeed, most agriculturally based developing societies as well have maintained structures and processes that were essentially *legal* in their conceptualization. The assumption was widespread that the integrity of a society and its capacity for dispensing justice could be measured in terms of a government's adherence to the "rule of law." Few of us would choose to live within a lawless system or within a system that dispensed justice more unevenly than is already common practice in many countries today. And in recent years the courts and other legal institutions have made constructive efforts to defend human rights—enforcing school integration, admitting class-action suits, and otherwise addressing critical social problems. To a considerable extent, however, such intervention by the courts may be accepted as evidence of the insensitivity of executive and legislative institutions, as well as of the public at large, to widespread human needs. In a properly functioning democracy, court intervention should be necessary only in anomalous cases.

Many traditional approaches are simply not adequate for some of the problems that confront us today. The difficulty is not only that legal "solutions" to rising crime rates, for example, are often not effective, that legal "fees" are often way out of proportion to the services rendered, or that the underlying purpose of the civil suit is frequently abused. The problem lies even deeper; it is embedded in the very structure of contemporary society. A large part of today's legislation is written by lawyers, conceived in narrow legal frameworks, and couched in legal language dating back to the Middle Ages or earlier. On the executive side of government, much of our policymaking, decision making, administrative control, and enforcement is carried out by lawyers trained within the same traditional contexts. Legal codes and procedures depend heavily upon adversary conceptualizations, relationships, procedures, and judgments, whereas many of our most critical and challenging problems may not be susceptible to this kind of approach. Often the conflict is not between right and wrong, but between two rights that appear to be at odds with each other. Issues involving economic growth and environmental protection offer a case in point. How is the day-to-day economic well-being of a society to be reconciled with environmental controls and the preservation of our vital resources? Any number of other seemingly contradictory issues are now painfully familiar. How are the risks of a nuclear accident to be weighed against growing demands for energy? How much welfare can the economy support? As the society grows older, how are we to balance the expanding needs of those on social security against the tax load of the proportionately smaller number of citizens in their working years?

As often as not, such problems cannot be settled optimally in terms of I-win-you-lose settlements or even in terms of absolute, one-shot compromises. There is a need for a considerable amount of legal reconceptualization and for the development of more or less "self-regulating" arrangements. Some prototype mechanisms are already in operation: a polluting enterprise is progressively taxed, for example, according to the amount of damage it does, and the accumulating revenue is then used to develop pollution control devices or to refurbish the environment. Similarly, as a resource such as oil is depleted, the consumption is progressively taxed and the proceeds used to locate new resources or develop substitutes. These are illustrative arrangements wherein some combination of legislated inverse-feedback arrangements is likely to provide more effective regulation, over the longer run, than many of the relatively inflexible statutes and enforcement procedures that are currently relied upon. Other contradictions—such as the demand for nuclear safety as opposed to the demand for more energy—may be more difficult to solve, requiring experimentation and perhaps bold innovation that will provide ways for meeting requirements on both sides of such issues.

It seems doubtful, however, that the more serious and potentially disruptive conflicts and instabilities within contemporary societies can be corrected without major alterations in our values and practices which determine the allocation of resources and benefits. Widespread achievement and maintenance of social, political, and legal equality may require as a necessary, but almost certainly not sufficient, condition a more equitable economic base than has so far been achieved in any state-level society.

Over recent decades a number of societies have tried to achieve economic and social equity through violent revolution and coercive administration. In most cases the results have been at best uneven, and advances in social and economic equity have often been secured at high cost in terms of legal safeguards and political equity. By and large, the leaders of these revolutionary movements have accepted as "scientifically" axiomatic, if not as articles of faith, the propositions that, on the one hand, the rich, powerful, and exploitative elements of society will not relinquish their advantages without violent struggle, and, on the other hand, that it is precisely through struggle, frequently coercive and violent, that the masses of people achieve higher levels of social, economic, or political consciousness. Historical events of the last half century, in the Soviet Union and elsewhere, cast some doubt on the validity of such assumptions, however. Few of us would deny that those with power, wealth, and other advantages are reluctant to give them up or that there are many lessons to be learned from the experiencing of violence. It is almost a cliché, however, that violence tends to generate counterviolence, and that coercion, even for a supposedly good cause, presupposes advantages of power and other inequities—often the first step in the replacement of an old ruling elite with a new ruling elite. The fundamental question raised by this book is whether there may not be more constructive, longer-lasting ways—derived from observations of the human condition reaching back to our remotest beginnings—whereby mass learning can be facilitated and new levels of social, economic, and political consciousness more rapidly and peacefully achieved.

Three Approaches to Utopia Building

As soon as we move from criticizing an existing society to designing a whole new one—or even to creating new component organizations and institutions for the old society—we run into vexing problems. A society with a history and traditions, or a component organization or institution that has become enmeshed in a society's customs and traditions, can prolong its existence long after it has ceased to serve the purpose for which it was initiated. An established society does not normally collapse until it has been leveled by revolution or conquest, or until its most vital functions have ceased to operate. A new society or institution does not enjoy this advantage. On the contrary, even though it may appear on paper to be a desirable structure for performing a much-needed task, a new society or institution is likely to be extremely difficult to set in motion and even more difficult to preserve. Most new organizations fail unless they are sustained in some way by an established and strongly functioning arm of society. No new model is likely to survive for very long unless it demonstrates a capability for performing notably better than existing institutions a function for which there is great demand.

There are three primary ways in which alternate institutions for the future can be created, experimented with, and tested. One involves the establishment of new, real-world organizations and institutions to accomplish specific tasks within existing societies. A second approach calls for the drafting of pencil-and-paper utopias in the grand tradition of Plato and Sir Thomas More. And, in keeping with contemporary technological developments, the third way involves the generation and testing of alternate designs with the aid of computer simulation and forecasting techniques. Whichever of these approaches we prefer, we can draw upon the three utopias or models described in Chapter Four. In so doing, we will be forced to consider what we want in the utopia we design—what types of competition are to be encouraged; what distributions of resources, benefactions, power, and influence are to be considered optimal; and so forth. The assumptions we choose, the values we apply, and the characteristics of the processes we set in motion will have powerful effects upon human outcomes within each utopia we formulate.

Utopias can be designed for many different levels of society from the individual and the family to the community, the nation, or humankind as a whole. In recent years people of various ages and walks of life have established and experimented with new, real-world organizations and institutions within established societies. These undertakings range from communes of many sorts to consumer cooperatives, worker-owned factories, and various mutual-aid organizations for therapeutic human rehabilitation.

Many of these organizations are essentially economic or political in nature and result from dissatisfactions that arise from inflation, depression, unemployment, bureaucratic frustrations, and alienation or fatigue engendered by societies over which people feel they have little or no control. Other new organizations spring from deep sociological and psychological dislocations. Alcoholics Anonymous, for example, is a voluntaristic organization, intensely participatory, democratic, and self-regulating, designed to help individual members to cope effectively with compulsions and other pathologies that have been progressively disrupting their own lives and those of their close associates. Central to the effectiveness of such organizations is the assumption that the best therapy for an alcoholic, drug addict, or compulsive gambler is provided by a fellow sufferer who has succeeded in surmounting his or her problem. It is worth serious consideration whether or not, in the long run, organizations of this sort may not be more effective than courts, police, prisons, and other coercive institutions for the control of a whole range of destructive behaviors.

The tendency toward creation of new organizations and institutions reflects, in part at least, a widespread dissatisfaction, if not disillusionment, with things as they are. Governments, societies, and sometimes whole civilizations collapse to the extent that they become incapable of meeting fundamental human needs. Conversely, the societies that survive over the long run are likely to be those which—as compared with other societies of the same era—most effectively meet the needs of their people.

Cybernetic Models and Possibilities for Societal Planning

Two of the factors responsible for the new revolution or system break, 1) cybernetic systems of communication and 2) the harnessing of unprecedented amounts of energy, may also enhance our ability to cope with the changes we face. The understanding of cybernetic relationships opens new possibilities for planning which previously has been dependent, both conceptually and in operational terms, upon the prevailing technology and level of organization. Given the pervasiveness, complexity, and depth of world problems, it seems evident that mere tinkering around the edges is not likely to see us through them safely. The task is to reconsider, reassess, and readjust the functioning of societies from roots to lofty foliage. But institutional changes of such magnitude are not easily accomplished.

Our difficulties arise from both the physical and social environments. To the extent that we interfere substantially in the mechanisms of nature—clearing forests, debilitating the soil, exhausting local water supplies, polluting the atmosphere, spreading pesticides, and so forth—we confront the necessity for providing substitute modes of stability. Similarly, to the extent that we maintain institutions that benefit some people at the expense of others, we may expect our societies to suffer severe crises and disruptions. At the same time, the dismantling of existing institutions is likely to create disruptions of its own, especially if the underlying inequities or other malfunctions are not identified and corrected. Revolutionaries of the past often have not given much practical thought to the replacement of the institutions they have smashed or uprooted. In view of the destructive power of modern weaponry, as well as the delicate balance of life-sustaining forces in the world today, we can scarcely afford miscalculations or missteps—although a frightening number are almost certain to be made.

On the band and tribal level, human beings planned in terms of the changes in season, availability of edible plants, and movements of game. In several parts of the world, where large-scale irrigation played a central role in the agricultural revolution, planning became much more sophisticated. In order to acquire, impound, and distribute huge quantities of water, early specialists had to develop a relatively complex body of knowledge involving weather prediction, the organizing and maintaining of complicated logistics, the deployment and feeding of gang labor, the control of floods, and the keeping of land records. The industrial revolution necessitated even broader and more intensive planning. Large-scale production required investments and other movements of capital, the building and maintenance of factories, acquisition of resources, inventory controls, and development of new machines. Among the consequences of the industrial revolution were changes in the social system that required new types of planning. Urbanization gave rise to city planning and the development of designed suburbs.

Increasingly, social welfare programs became an integral part of industrial societies. After World War II economic and technological assistance programs were founded on the assumption that it is possible to stimulate and control the growth of whole societies in systematic ways. By the middle 1960s it was becoming increasingly clear, however, that most planners had an inadequate understanding of growth processes in their own societies, to say nothing of the economic and social dynamics of other countries.

The systems of allocating and distributing resources that emerged during the industrial era encouraged and, in turn, were fed by economic growth, which was accepted as the dominant function of the society. In virtually all societies economic growth has become the goal, rather than the means, of allocation systems. Today the success of a society, whether industrialized or still developing, is measured by overall GNP (gross national product) rather than in terms of any number of other possible indicators.

Planning has usually assumed the feasibility and desirability of growth. But the values and goals that evolved in the industrial era (and served it so well) are becoming counterproductive to the stability of contemporary societies. In the face of rising populations and resource constraints, the pursuit of unqualified economic growth and consumption may be an invitation to world turmoil and possible catastrophe. The benefits of modern technology may have to be distributed more widely before economic growth in the developed countries can be substantially expanded.

Economic growth has always exacted penalties in one form or another, but often the costs have not been visible in those societies that have achieved abundance. The social and environmental costs and benefits of a public policy are often exceedingly difficult to assess. To get at them properly we have to confront the master variables—population, technology, and resources—in order to see how they are combining, what the implications are if present trends persist, what viable alternatives can be identified, and how each such alternative might be achieved. Frequently the costs and benefits of a public policy are poorly defined, and much confusion arises because the costs sometimes precede the benefits and the benefits sometimes precede the costs. Other difficulties arise in determining who pays the costs and who receives the benefits.

With improved methodological tools, assessing the policies and identifying the distribution of costs and benefits may be possible, but there is no objectively "correct" arrangement of rewards and penalties. With these new tools, however, we should be able to generate large numbers of alternate models, making the different arrays of costs and benefits, together with their distributions, fully explicit.

Experimenting with the Future

Nowhere in this book have I indicated what specific type of system will be most appropriate for the future—capitalist, socialist, communist, a "mixed" system of one sort or another, or something altogether new. This restraint has been deliberate. Such labels as capitalist, socialist, and so forth can be semantic traps that keep us from effective thinking. In condemning several of the highly centralized, politically coercive so-called socialist states that have appeared since World War I, for example, some of us overlook a wide range of possibilities for the development of decentralized, more voluntaristic cooperatives and collectives. Similarly, in castigating the massive, increasingly centralized, economically coercive capitalist societies that exist in parts of the world today, others of us ignore possibilities for smaller, decentralized, more socially sensitive free-enterprise arrangements that might be developed in local communities. As we confront the world and its problems today, it is difficult to identify *any* system that appears to be fully adequate for the challenges we face. The more carefully we examine the plight of humankind today, the less blindly partisan our attitudes are likely to be. In such circumstances, it seems more useful for us to focus on human problems and relationships and social, political, and economic processes rather than on a particular ideology.

The three utopias examined in Chapter Four illustrate some of the trade-offs and dilemmas. Through intense competition, the tooth and claw model disciplines the population as well as the marketplace and, up to some threshold, gets things done with considerable efficiency—and human cost. By constraining part of the competition and providing even the "unfit" with some minimum of human welfare, the competition-welfare model serves humanistic values up to a point. But under these more relaxed constraints, considerable numbers of less efficient, even "unfit" organizations survive. As for those individuals who cannot or will not conform to the competition aspects of the system, there are limited possibilities open to them. Large numbers of them want more, get discouraged, and drop out—or make careers out of milking the system. As for the multilevel, equal-access model, it is not a panacea. On the contrary, it faces the worst paradox of all: in the search for a mechanism for enforcing equal access and assuring sufficient product yield, there may be a temptation, even an "imperative," to borrow coercive features from the other two models; but to the extent that this is done, some measure of equal access and democratic universalism almost certainly will be lost.

Previously I have suggested the importance of intentional social, economic, and political experimentation on local levels. This might include the development of new ways of relating people to people and people to resources and also of solving a whole range of vital access problems (access to critical resources, information, benefactions, decision and control) for people whose access is now seriously impeded. These are immediate, practical approaches to the future. We will now turn to some of the more theoretical approaches to the solving of our long-range problems.

Relatively simple approaches to the future may involve the writing of plausible utopias that try to solve some of our more critical problems, or, alternatively, the construction of very simple data projections that can be done with pencil and paper. More spectacular possibilities may lie just over the horizon, however. Indeed, a computerized system recently developed at the University of Illinois—bearing the name PLATO, appropriately enough—may provide a prototype for unprecedented approaches to utopia building.

In its present form the PLATO system encompasses a centralized bank, located at the University of Illinois, which contains an extensive array of demographic data for most of the countries of the world, a more limited but continually expanding amount of economic data, and various computer programs. The user is provided with a terminal, which can be plugged into a telephone line connecting it with the central bank. This terminal, in turn, consists of a typewriter-style keyboard and a graphics assembly, which looks very much like a large television screen. The user calls up the data he wants—the population of the United States at ten-year intervals since 1800, for example—and watches it appear either in statistical form or as a rising line on a graph emerging before his eyes. Having obtained these historical data, the user may then ask for an expert's prediction of the U.S. population at ten-year intervals from now until, for example, the year 2100. But the user need not accept the expert's prediction. On the contrary, he may try out his own prediction—in the form of a constant growth rate, varying rates of growth, even zero growth—and watch the consequences at ten-year intervals over the next 50, 100, or 200 years. Having done this, the user may now call for the GNP of the United States, go through a similar exercise, combine the population and GNP data to provide per capita data, and so forth.

Such techniques are still in their early infancy, but they are almost certain to develop rapidly over the next few years. We can imagine only a few years hence special desks equipped with typewriter-like keyboards and using cassette tapes, or their equivalent, being made available not only to national leaders in public and private sectors but also to libraries, universities, colleges, high schools, even secondary schools. Each desk will be capable of ordering, analyzing, and displaying on a screen vast amounts of demographic, social, economic, and political data. Anyone who can ask questions and type them in can obtain answers about the past, present, and future. In a few minutes' time, a sixth-grade student can watch a hundred years of population growth, increasing resource demands, intricate trade patterns, pollution trends, or spiraling military budgets unfold on the screen. If he or she wants to assume the continuation of past trends into the next 15, 30, or 50 years, it will be possible to call them up on the screen and see some of the consequences. Then the student will be able to "reduce" population growth and observe some of *those* consequences; decrease consumption; divide the whole world product evenly among everyone; or bring the world population up to the United States' per capita level and observe the consequences. All of us should be able to learn much faster as we are able to see difficult problems springing into motion across PLATO-like screens.

But PLATO deals only with numbers, you may object. What about human values? What about moral choices? We have already suggested some of the ways in which quality is related to quantity—how numbers of people and amounts of resources can affect our demands and values, how changes in technology can influence our wants and even modify a whole culture. The availability and allocation of resources and benefits are critical considerations. Politics has long been defined in terms of who gets what, when, and how. This definition seemed adequate as long as goods and services were perceived as being created and exchanged in the absence of any direct ecological constraints. Today it is increasingly evident, however, that politics (as well as economics and ethics) refers in even more subtle ways to crucial decisions by human beings about the control, allocation, and distribution of resources and the manipulation and utilization of the natural environment. Since resources and the planetary environment are finite, the growth rates and size of human populations are basic variables in our future, as are the levels of our technology and the ways in which we consume our resources. Demands for resources vary with changes in population and technology, and the limits of available resources change with the level and characteristics of technology.

Such possibilities for graphic, computerized analysis may become much more than mere classroom exercises. To understand the social, economic, political, and environmental impacts of future changes in population, technology, and resource availabilities, government leaders and their advisers throughout the world need to examine changing ratios of these variables over a considerable segment of history—the last 100 years, where feasible, and for newer countries or countries without earlier statistical records, the last 20 or 25 years at least. Even if these data are merely plotted year by year without further analysis, they will provide a vivid picture of the direction in which we are headed. If we continue these plots another 20 or 30 years into the future, we will obtain a picture not only of how ecology bears on social, economic, and political systems, but also of how politics must increasingly involve the regulation and management of population growth and distribution, of resource usages and allocations, and of technological advancement and applications (including the control of pollution).

Vastly more powerful generations of PLATO-like systems might enable us to monitor and analyze ongoing world trends. How has the international system been operating over the previous two or three decades? Where and in what social as well as physical environments have coups, revolutions, and wars taken place? How have policies in one's own country improved or worsened the world situation? What are today's most serious problems, and what choices of action are available? These are only a few of a wide array of questions that might be asked.

Are we indulging in pipe dreams? On the contrary, the functional equivalents of our imaginary desk unit may well be a reality within the next five to ten years. Such tools, made available to everyone everywhere, could vastly speed up social learning and possibly contribute over a generation or more to futures that we can scarcely even imagine from today's perspective. It might then be possible to identify conflicts before they get out of control and suggest cooperative, creative ways of resolving them.

A further suggestion has been made—perhaps an absurdly utopian one—for the use of modern technology to help us to visualize the world and our place in it. During the Vietnam War television was able to bring jungle skirmishes into the American living room. Soon the possibilities may be vastly greater. Suppose that the planet were ringed with satellites comparable to those that now assist in forecasting the weather. Equipped with sensitive photographic equipment, these satellites, via a reserved channel, would display shifting views of the world (day and night) on earthbound television screens. Sitting before television sets, whether in urban apartments, isolated farm houses, village squares, or jungle compounds, people at any time could see the earth, sometimes from afar, sometimes close up. Operating randomly, the cameras might zoom in, now on one country, now on another, revealing storms over land or sea, urban traffic, vehicles on a freeway, carts enroute to rural markets, a flood here, a drought area there, a village on fire, a war in progress. In this way all of us could see with our own eyes again and again—at the flick of a switch—that we do indeed live on one small planet sailing through space. And to the extent that we are able thus to bring world events into the living room, we may begin to sense, without dependence on the written word, how we as individuals fit into the larger human society. We may then learn things about ourselves, as well as about the rest of the world, that books could never convey.

The cybernetic revolution may thus allow us not only to keep track of vastly more information about our interactions with the world than ever before, but also to analyze it in graphic new ways (even to animate it) and make it visible around the world. Through communications satellites under international control, one can imagine a never-ending flow of visual information being distributed to schools, libraries, village squares, isolated trading stations—to every corner of the earth with a television set.

Any serious approach to utopia building and the generation of alternative courses of action requires a certain amount of prediction. Unfortunately, the use of this word tends to make people think of crystal balls or the reading of tea leaves. Obviously this is not what we intend. Although the development of computers and computer simulations has stimulated a new awareness of prediction as an element in policy for-

The Earth seen from space; photographed from artificial satellite, May 1970.

mation and planning, the fact remains that policy decisions have always implied some degree of prediction—some "if this, then probably that" assessment of outcome. The Marshall Plan was based upon the prediction that systematic aid to European nations would reinvigorate their economies and halt the spread of communism into Central and Western Europe. Viewed in retrospect, this prediction seems to have been generally sound, at least for the first decades after World War II. By contrast, the basic prediction inherent in Khrushchev's decision to establish long-range missiles in Cuba, for example, was much less accurate. Obviously, there is nothing magic in this kind of prediction. Even the weatherman is correct only part of the time, and international politics is considerably more perverse than the weather. Yet, predictive skills can be improved. Computers and computer simulations will be able to provide the investigator or planner with a new ability to experiment with complex systems and obtain a feel for how these systems work.

Until recently, most people have assumed that trends of the recent past will continue into the near future. Prediction has been based on what is "likely to happen" and has proceeded with a kind of linear planning along given tracks and within a given framework. But increasingly, a new concern for worldwide problems involving population, technology transfers, pollution, inflation, and issues of food, oil, and other resources has broadened the planning function to include the search for the underpinnings of a world culture—new sets of values to be implemented and new, flexible responses to events on a rapidly changing planet. The concept of a world culture does not preclude the survival of ethnic minorities or national cultures. On the contrary, the protection and enrichment of local enclaves, languages, and cultures might well be encouraged within the larger, more universal framework. The idea of a world culture would presuppose, however, that the survival and future well-being of ethnic enclaves and whole nationalities must depend upon a secure humankind pursuing self-fulfillment on a flourishing planet.

How are we to achieve a worldwide transformation of this order? What values must be identified, disseminated, inculcated, and invoked? With what innovative, flexible, creative attitudes and actions can people everywhere learn while responding to events in a rapidly changing world? In an article entitled "How Men Can Shape Their Futures" (*Futures*, March 1971), biochemist John Platt likens the process of change to the driving of a vehicle. He believes that social processes should not be compared to a "railroad train running on fixed tracks to an inevitable destination," however, "but rather to a wagon train of settlers moving

Kanesville—Missouri River Crossing—1856 by William Henry Jackson.

across the country towards the frontier, in an ongoing collective search for a better place to live." Like a vehicle, a society at any given moment is "at a particular place with a particular direction of motion determined by its previous history." The problem is, Platt asserts, how far down the road can the driver see and how much control over his vehicle does he have. From Platt's perspective, we can divide the road of the future into three periods of time. Depending on the speed of the vehicle, there is a short time ahead during which the driver, however well he can see, can do little to change course. "We hit the dog on the road or our society gets into war, regardless of the most heroic efforts to swerve away." Here Platt refers to what is commonly called lag time in planning and decision making. Once the Japanese task force was launched against Pearl Harbor, it would have been difficult for the Japanese leadership to call it off. Galloping inflation cannot be slowed down overnight; months or years may be required. For a society like the United States to switch from reliance on oil to reliance on coal may require a decade or two.

Beyond the immediate future, the possibilities for changing policy and outcome are increased somewhat. As Platt suggests in terms of a vehicle, "the momentum-physics of the next half-second from now is steadily replaced, in anticipating future seconds, by the cybernetics of goal-directed steering." Under such conditions, Platt continues, " 'predictions' cease to be predictions and become something more like 'advice' or 'warnings' so that the alert society, or the alert driver, can avoid the foreseen dangers or choose the desirable directions that have just become apparent. For this period, the problem is not to predict the future but to change it." There is time to change direction, to avoid a pothole, or even to turn a corner. For the national leader and his advisers, there is time to organize a Marshall Plan or to participate in the drafting of a seabed treaty.

The third time period extends into the more distant future, a span of uncertainty which, declares Platt, "is too far off and too dependent on intervening hazards and our intervening responses for present planning or steering to be relevant except in terms of very general directions." This ultimate period of uncertainty is like the stretch "after the next bend in the road." For the national planner or decision maker, this period may lie a decade or more in the future. Now only broad goals or general guidelines can be set—tentative plans for obtaining and distributing sufficient water for the nation's needs in 1990 or assessing the world food and population situation as it is likely to be at the turn of the century. The details for how to get where we are going have to be worked out as we move along and are able to see better.

Through causal modeling, simulation, and forecasting techniques, the analyst or policymaker can infer with a high degree of confidence what values a given society has acted upon with some consistency over a period of 30 years or more in the past. From 1946 through 1975, for example, we can identify and plot the major trends that have taken place and can also postulate what *societal* values have prevailed and have actually been invoked. We can even test and calibrate our tools by inserting historical data for part of this period of time, such as from 1946 to 1951, and forecasting the trends (as if we had not already established them) through 1975. At that point it is possible to compare the forecasted trends with the real-world trends and calculate the error. Assuming that major trends of the past (and the values that produced them) will continue into the future, we can then make forecasts for 30, 40, or 50 years into the real future. Having achieved this baseline projection on the basis of very explicit, though perhaps unrealistic, assumptions about the future, it is possible to introduce alternate values—different overall investment patterns, demographic or economic growth rates, national budgetary allocations, income distributions, and the like—and observe the probable outcomes. In this way, thousands of alternative futures can be generated with all assumptions and each introduction of a new value recorded and made explicit. Not only can we introduce a new value in country *A*'s decision making and watch the outcome for *A*, we can also trace the consequences in terms of other countries and introduce hypothetical changes in them as well. For instance, we can plot the interactive relationships between the military expenditure patterns of the United States and the Soviet Union since 1946. We can also determine for each country the patterns of interrelation between military expenditures and other trends, such as industrial production, health expenditures, oil consumption, or international trade patterns. It is then possible to introduce hypothetical changes in Soviet military expenditures, cutting them in half, for example, and then observe the alterations that take place in the related trends—both in the USSR and in the United States.

Through modeling, simulation, and forecasting, a number of difficult questions can be addressed in disciplined fashion. In what circumstances, for what purposes, and within what limitations should economic growth be encouraged? How is it to be furthered? What are the expected benefits? What are the possible damaging side effects? Under what circumstances can seemingly peaceful and constructive activities such as trade, economic aid, and transfers of technology contribute to conflict, violence, or other undesirable outcomes? How do domestic growth and foreign relations affect each other? With respect to any particular issue, what is the relationship between the interests of a given nation and the interests of humanity as a whole? To the extent that answers to these questions can be found, value choices concerning future policy can be made more rationally. In order to make wise decisions now, a fuller understanding of the probable consequences of making or *not* making particular choices is badly needed.

With arrangements for adequate monitoring, analysis, and distribution of information, heads of states and their advisers, leaders in private sectors, and, most important, the citizenry at large could have richer, more systematic, and more dynamic information with which to balance immediate or short-term benefits against probable medium- and long-range costs. All of us would be better able to see how each policy alternative reverberates through the international system and through component nations, including our own. With some reasonable assessments of both costs and benefits, and with some indication of who among us is likely to gain and who to lose, we might perceive more clearly what trade-offs are involved with each alternative, including trade-offs between short-term and long-term interests.

Historically, people have frequently fought for territory, sea and land routes, and various basic resources. Often, too, population pressures have contributed to major wars. There is considerable evidence, however, that desires for power, prestige, or dominance in many subtle forms have also contributed to the outbreak of war and have been closely connected with the availability of resources, markets, cheap labor, or strategic advantages. Frequently the aggressor appears to be a rapidly growing and seemingly successful nation—a nation undergoing an upsurge in economic, technological, and population growth—whose leaders (and populace) become obsessed with achieving and maintaining first place, or at least a dominant position, no matter what the cost. Or the aggressor may be a declining great power determined to preserve its dominance.

From the dawn of history war has been available and recognized, in most societies, as one means—often, indeed, as a venerable institution—for resolving major conflicts arising from a wide variety of circumstances. This is no longer the case. A pessimistic appraisal of the situation today suggests a seedbed for catastrophe. One may entertain serious doubts whether the competitive, often violent nation-state system as it now exists is any longer safe for the human race. The danger is great that, in some angry crisis of the future, the leaders on one side or the other may be pushed to the point where a nuclear strike seems rational—perhaps the only thinkable course of action left. Or, on a local level—somewhere, sometime—an embittered guerrilla band, or even a lone fanatic, may carry nuclear blackmail to an ultimate conclusion.

We have the capacity to pursue rational solutions if we choose to do so. But our tendency is often to grope, switch, and procrastinate before making a major change. The magnitude of the tasks that confront us requires considerable lead time for formulating effective solutions. Even if we slammed the brakes on world population growth and conspicuous consumption tomorrow, it would require decades, even generations, for the full consequences to be realized. And the difficulties of controlling nuclear weapons, protecting the environment, and bringing backward economies up to a tolerable level are already manifest.

The task we confront is at once political, economic, and technological. It is also demographic, social, psychological, and ethical. Technology in a broad sense—the organization and application of human knowledge, skills, and tools on many levels of activity—provides us with unprecedented alternatives and opportunities *provided* we learn quickly enough to make wise use of them. Selectively applied to our problems, these unfolding technological developments can enhance the possibilities for self-fulfillment. Unfortunately, they can also be used to increase misery and even bring about the destruction of the human race. The challenge confronting us all is whether or not, individually and collectively, we can choose courses of action on a day-to-day basis that are rational and moral for humankind as well as for our own immediate interests.

Possibilities for New Solutions

Over the next 25 to 100 years the lives and fortunes of humankind are likely to be altered in profound ways by a wide range of different technologies. Some of these technologies are already available to us; others may be developed within the lifetimes of our children or grandchildren. 1) Nuclear power and weaponry are already commonplace. 2) Space exploration has barely begun. Spaceships will carry instruments, if not human beings themselves, into regions that were penetrated previously only by astronomers with the aid of their telescopes or other earth-based probing devices. 3) Satellite networks are already providing "instant" verbal and visual communications over much of the earth, and there are enormous possibilities for refinement and expansion. 4) Supersonic transport is already in operation, but in time we may have rocket-type, high-altitude shuttles capable of bringing all major cities of the world within commuting distance of each other.

5) Cybernetic control systems may be expected to operate vast industrial complexes, perform many routine administrative functions in business and government at all levels, and greatly enhance engineering, urban planning and development, and so forth. 6) Biomedical technologies may prolong life, enhance capacities for learning, manipulate genetic structure, and perhaps even create life itself. 7) In addition we may find ways to tap massive amounts of primary energy from the oceans or directly from the sun. Each of these developments will create serious problems as well as benefits. Each will strain existing social, economic, and political systems in unprecedented ways. The challenge will be how to control them and use them to the advantage of all people throughout the world.

To a large extent human affairs on all levels of organization from the local community to the nation and the world at large are still regulated and disciplined primarily by economic or political competition and conflict. Consequently, as social scientists Charles Lave and James March point out in their book *An Introduction to Models in the Social Sciences*, "A common first reaction to solving any problem is to choose coercion—pass a law or issue an order." This tends to be true not only with respect to drugs, crime, and many other difficult problems on a local level, but also with respect to conflicts and disorders on national and international levels. Accordingly, a common response to mass poverty, revolution, and war is to propose the establishment of a world government. But such a solution, in addition to being difficult to achieve, might well present serious problems of its own. Is the world government to have a coercive force at its disposal, and if so, who is to control it? The history of coercive government at the national level does not commend a government of force at the world level as a solution.

Rather than primary reliance on coercion, according to Lave and March, we may find ways of solving many of our problems through the development of societies that provide more indirect, decentralized incentives than we are currently accustomed to. Since most of us have been born into highly competitive, more or less coercive societies, it is difficult for us to imagine how such incentives might be made available. *The fundamental objective would be to develop communities and whole societies that would reward mutual assistance rather than competition and conflict.* Such a development need not mean that we eradicate the competitive spirit, but that we apply it to sports, the arts, entertainment, and public welfare rather than to the acquisition of resources, wealth, and power. On a day-to-day basis such a mutual-assistance society might be expected to favor 1) individual activities rewarding to the larger community, 2) community activities allowing the individual optimal possibilities for self-fulfillment, and 3) activities between individuals, between groups, and between national societies allowing each to reinforce the other rather than to destructively compete or conflict.

Technology by itself will not achieve such a society for us. Development along these lines clearly begins with the feelings, ideas, values, and moral choices of individuals and groups working in concert. But technology *can* provide us with useful tools. Modern communications can exacerbate our conflicts, for example, but perhaps they can also bring us closer together. Our Paleolithic and Neolithic ancestors kept order in their band and tribal societies partly because, living face-to-face as they did, secrecy and plotting were difficult. Increasingly, today, the priorities tend to be upside down: powerful individuals, private organizations, and nations control more and more information and are protected by more and more secrecy, whereas the individual at large risks losing the limited amount of privacy he or she has come to cherish.

By yielding undue protection to self-serving activities of powerful corporations in the private sector, to governments contemplating exploitation or aggression, and to dissident groups plotting nuclear blackmail, such secrecy endangers not only the individual, but all countries of the world, and mankind as well. For individual human beings a sense of self-fulfillment requires a certain amount of privacy, and this should be safeguarded. The preservation of individual integrity may require equal access to privacy as well as to information. But particularly in the nuclear age, the combination of power and secrecy is likely to become increasingly dangerous. Our future security may require public surveillance of all governmental offices and trusts, all private firms and combinations affecting people's welfare, and all concentrations of power whatsoever. Perhaps the satellite information system mentioned earlier as an educational tool might also enhance the security of everyone by bringing people out of the shadows of secrecy.

These are only a few of the many considerations we might keep in mind while constructing models for the future. We will all be starting from the baseline of our own personal backgrounds, experiences, assumptions, values, expectations, and preferences. The more seriously we consider the utopias we are able to develop, the more we will learn about ourselves and other people, and the more sensitive we will become to the difficulties involved in finding solutions to the problems that confront us. Then, as Lave and March point out, after developing each model, the truly important task is "to delight in finding out what is wrong with it."

As a starter, here are two crude, extreme projections of what the world might look like a hundred years from now:

Optimistic

Worldwide, consensual, pluralistic, but effective international networks of institutions for resolving international disputes, with decentralized regional units for regional conflicts. Universally sanctioned countervailing measures for heading off disorders and potentially dangerous confrontations—some economic, some social, political, or judicial. National armed forces as obsolete as private armed forces are today. Today's vast military technology converted for ocean and space exploration and colonization and other constructive enterprises on an international scale.

International agencies regulating access to resources and technology on a more equal basis than exists today.

Population levels regulated by region in accordance with available resources and levels of productivity. Loosening of national barriers to allow free travel and immigration correlated with inducements to attract populations where a labor force is needed or where the environment can support larger numbers of people.

Unrestricted, worldwide, lifetime opportunities for education and training without respect to age, race, creed, color, or economic background. Intercontinental, intercultural, and international programs for agricultural, economic, technological, and scientific development along lines that will provide relatively equal access and conserve resources.

Internationally regulated audio and video communications networks serving as a worldwide free and open marketplace for news, information, knowledge, skills, and culture. Strict safeguards against possible monolithic control by any single interest group.

Decentralization, division, and dispersion of governmental decision and control—according to function—on local (village, town, city, locality), provincial, national, regional, and world-

Pessimistic

Nuclear blackmail; cataclysmic nuclear or biological war; bootlegging of satchel-sized nuclear weapons by Mafia-type organizations or guerrilla groups. Proliferation of more conventional, less devastating, yet destructive and disruptive wars on land, at sea, in the air, and in space; wars over control of resources or in defense of trade routes; generations of cold war; nuclear or other blackmail from military bases in space; ideological warfare through control of communications satellites.

Vast population surpluses and famine coupled with resource scarcities and accumulating pollution, at least in some parts of the world. Industrialized nations short of energy; developing nations short of food.

Rich nations getting richer; poor nations getting poorer; within nations the well-to-do majority gaining while the depressed minorities become more depressed. Economic warfare and blackmail. Wars of liberation in underdeveloped areas and endemic guerrilla conflicts threatening to escalate.

Proliferation of conflicts along a single line or several lines of cleavage; that is, the currently richer, more secure, technologically more advanced, healthier, longer-living, white minority of the world versus the poorer, less secure, slower developing, less healthy, shorter-living majority of nonwhites.

Inflation, monetary crises, unemployment, crime waves, vigilante organizations, and ad hoc justice.

Cybernetic control of audio and video communications networks around the world by a single autocratic power, by two or three deeply antagonistic superpowers, or by a coalition of superpowers. Secret computerized governmental and private data banks on individuals and groups suspected of dissidence. Proliferation of electronic information, surveillance, and management devices controlled by special interest groups.

wide levels. Encouragement of cultural diversity. Fundamental sovereignty residing in the individual. Local communities managing all affairs that can be decided and controlled on that level. Only issues that require wider decision or control delegated to progressively higher levels.

Worldwide international functions limited to the keeping of world peace; to international economic, technological, scientific, and communications regulation and development; to space exploration and control; and the like. Autonomy with respect to community and national affairs that do not impinge on the welfare and security of other communities or nations. Maximal provincial and local autonomy to counterbalance the power and authority of the national government (if national governments exist at all). Vastly increased citizen participation in government at all levels. With more leisure, citizens patterning themselves after the citizens of ancient Athens.

Supergovernments (or superindustries, super religious, benevolent, and protective associations, or super crime syndicates) controlling—with cybernetic aids—tax levying and collection, police surveillance, education and indoctrination, even political and/or religious belief without countervailing pressures and protections available to individuals and small groups; dictatorships with almost instantly retrievable master files and dossiers on each of its citizens with vital statistics, intelligence, and aptitude quotients, personality profiles, school credentials, employment and tax records, law violations, records of association memberships, and so forth; powerful bodies of professional specialists with the knowledge and power to lengthen or shorten life or to tamper surgically or genetically with life without public surveillance or accountability.

These two projections are meant to be suggestive, to stimulate our thinking, and neither one should be taken too seriously. Concepts of optimism and pessimism, not unlike the concepts of determinism, inevitability, and free will, can become semantic and even philosophical traps. The underlying truth is that we cannot even be certain who the optimists and pessimists are. Given the world situation today, is it optimistic to believe that there really are no serious problems, that things will somehow work themselves out, while rationalizing destructive competitions and large-scale violence in terms of an immutable human nature? And is it necessarily pessimistic to believe that humankind is currently plunging hell-bent toward catastrophe, but that if we will only step back a bit, observe, sort things out, think, marshall our creative capacities, and allow ourselves to learn, we may find new paths to better future outcomes?

Special efforts will have to be made on a worldwide basis if humankind is to avoid serious dislocations, economic warfare, violent struggles over access to vital resources, and eventual nuclear catastrophe. Fundamental to such efforts will be the task of incorporating within societies worldwide means for gathering, transmitting, and accurately evaluating information and knowledge as well as the capacity for acting on it (sometimes in new, unprecedented ways). Such a continuing process will require some means for ongoing cost-benefit analyses of alternatives, not just in monetary terms but, more importantly, in environmental and societal terms, and not merely in terms of particular societies but for people everywhere. The task will be to modify or replace old institutions *before* their malfunctioning does irreparable damage, to try out new methods and institutions on a tentative, carefully monitored basis, and to effect appropriate adjustments.

As suggested at the beginning of this book, prognostications about the future will depend a great deal upon assessments of human nature. My own view is that people are *not* wholly and immutably competitive or cooperative, compliant or aggressive, generous or selfish, peaceful or violent. We are at once the creatures of our genetic heritage, our geographic environments, our cultural backgrounds, the social, economic, and political structures of our respective societies, our personal experiences, and so forth. Sometimes we act the way we feel and sometimes we do not. Depending upon where we are, whom we are with, what we are doing to others, and what they are doing to us, we are susceptible to a whole range of feelings—some positive, some negative, some a mixture of both.

Normally, we have a great many possible choices, frequently more than we are aware of. Often we require a measure of repose in order to identify a creative, as opposed to a destructive, course of action. All of us, if we are so disposed, are capable of sublimation, of diverting a potentially destructive feeling or impulse into behavior that is constructive or at least less injurious to others. Whether we do so or not depends upon a great many factors, some inside us, some outside. Usually what we do is powerfully influenced by unnamed fears, by what we have done in the past, by what others have done to us, and by what we have learned from the interaction of the two. But new paths to better ways of dealing with each other are available—if only we can recognize them.

This book has tried to distinguish human beings and their individual feelings, minds, spirits, and potentials from the physical and social environments which in considerable part govern what they do. To one degree or another most of us today are severely constrained in what we think and do by the social webs in which we are entangled—just as our remote forebears were shaped by the physical environments of their time and by the social demands of their bands, tribes, chiefdoms, or early states and empires.

But we should not assume today that the modern state and the societies that have developed with it are necessarily any more permanent than their ancient and primeval predecessors. None of us need allow his or her feelings, thoughts, loyalties, or actions to be locked rigidly into contemporary social forms. There is a broad, deep, unexplored future extending out there before us waiting for our touch, and it will be molded by what we and our children do today, tomorrow, and thereafter. We can leave ourselves and the world to the fate of an untended commons, or we can seize upon the fifth great revolution and steer it toward a fulfilling future.

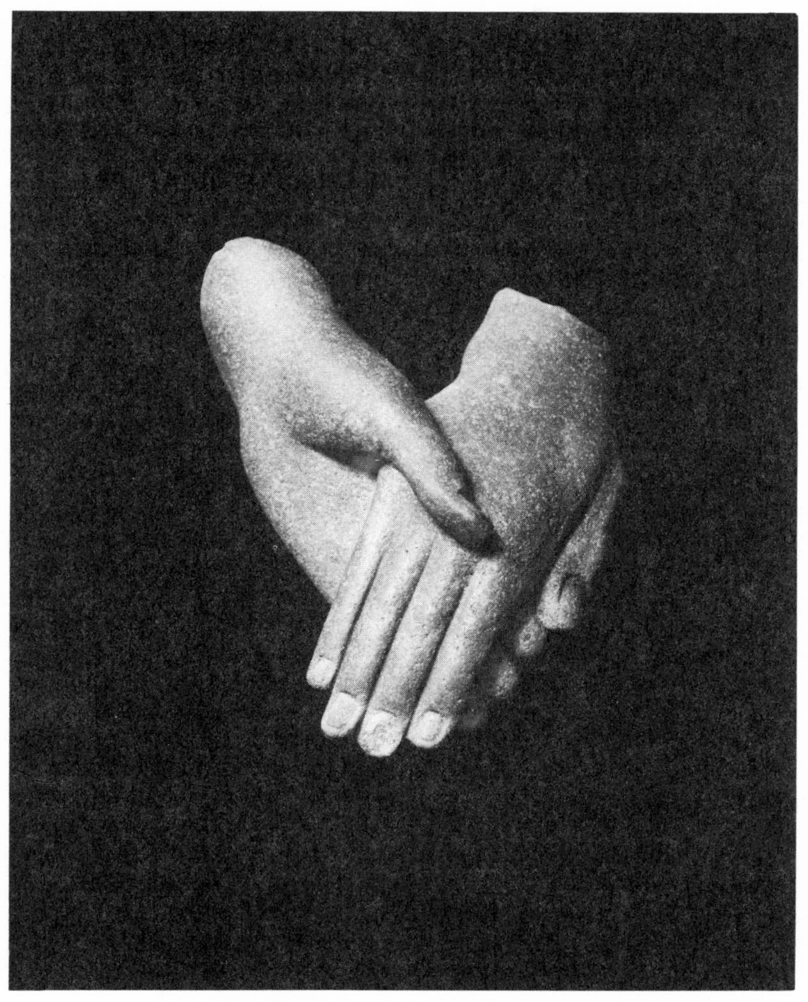

Clasped hands, quartzite fragment of an Amarna family group, from Amarna.

READER'S GUIDE

Chapter 1

The number of books and articles raising critical issues about the present and the future is too large for listing here. The following titles will provide a foundation for further reading.

Brown, Lester R. *World Without Borders*. New York: Vintage Books, 1973.

———. *In the Human Interest*. New York: Norton, 1974.

———. *By Bread Alone*. New York: Praeger, 1974.

Ehrlich, Paul R., Anne H. Ehrlich, and John Holdren. *Human Ecology*. San Francisco: W.H. Freeman, 1973.

Heilbroner, Robert L. *An Inquiry into the Human Prospect* (with "Second Thoughts"). New York: Norton, 1975.

Watt, Kenneth. *The Titanic Effect*. Stamford, Connecticut: Sinauer Associates, Inc., 1974.

Utopian communities and the concept of utopia are discussed in a great many different sources. The following books and articles touch upon the major points covered in Chapter 1.

Bakewell, Charles M. "Introduction," *Plato: The Republic*. New York: Charles Scribner's Sons, 1928.

Carden, Maren Lockwood. *Oneida: Utopian Community to Modern Corporation*. New York: Harper and Row, 1971.

Douglas, Dorothy W., and Catharine Der Pre Lumpkin. "Communistic Settlements," *Encyclopaedia of the Social Sciences*, vol. IV, pp. 96-101. New York: Macmillan, 1934.

Hinds, William Alfred. *American Communities*. New York: Corinth Books, 1961.

Mannheim, Karl. "Utopia," *Encyclopaedia of the Social Sciences*, vol. XV, p. 201. New York: Macmillan, 1934.

Skinner, B.F. *Walden Two*. London: Macmillan, 1960.

Chapter 2

Space is too limited here for the many reports that have appeared during the last decade or so on recent archaeological findings of early human remains. Two general books will provide the reader with manageable overviews of the long prehistory of human beings as a species.

Pfeiffer, John E. *The Emergence of Man*. New York: Harper and Row, 1969.

Young, J.Z. *An Introduction to the Study of Man*. New York: Oxford University Press, 1971.

For a basic theoretical discussion of the concept of sociocultural evolution, see

Campbell, Donald T. "Variation and Selective Retention in Socio-Cultural Evolution," *General Systems Yearbook* (1969), vol. XXV.

Applications of sociocultural evolutionary theory to the development of human social, economic, and political institutions are discussed by

Farb, Peter. *Man's Rise to Civilization as Shown by the Indians of North America from Primeval Times to the Coming of the Industrial Revolution.* New York: E.P. Dutton, 1972.

Service, Elman R. *Primitive Social Organization.* New York: Random House, 1962.

The following discussion of prestate economics provides insights which may help us to understand a number of contemporary social, economic, and political problems.

Sahlins, Marshall D. *Stone Age Economics.* Chicago: Aldine-Atherton Press, 1972.

For examples of how prestate societies maintained domestic cohesion and order, read

Fortes, Meyer, and E.E. Evans-Pritchard. *African Political Systems.* London: Oxford University Press, 1940.

Newell, William B. *Crime and Justice Among the Iroquois Nation.* Montreal: Caughnawage Historical Society, 1965.

Shepardson, Mary. "The Traditional Authority System of the Navajos," in Cohen, Ronald, and John Middleton. *Comparative Political Systems.* Garden City, New York: The Natural History Press, 1967.

Wissler, Clark. *The Social Life of the Blackfoot Indians.* Anthropological Papers of the American Museum of Natural History (1911), vol. 17, p. 164.

For a new and notably different perspective on pre-state warfare, see

Divale, William T. and Marvin Harris. "Population, Warfare and the Male Supremacist Complex," *American Anthropologist,* vol. 78, no. 3 (September, 1976), pp. 521–38.

Chapter 3

Theories and empirical data on the emergence and characteristics of state forms of organization will be found in

Carneiro, Robert L. "A Theory of the Origin of the State," *Science* (August 21, 1970), vol. 169, no. 3947, p. 733.

Drucker, Philip. "Rank, Wealth and Kinship in Northwest Coast Society," in McFeat, Tom (ed.). *Indians of the North Pacific Coast.* Toronto: McClelland and Stewart, Ltd., 1966.

Lowie, Robert H. "Political Organization Among the American Aborigines," in Cohn, Ronald, and John Middleton. *Comparative Political Systems.* Garden City, New York: The Natural History Press, 1967.

MacIver, Robert M. *The Modern State.* Oxford: Clarendon Press, 1926.

Schevill, Ferdinand. *Medieval and Renaissance Florence,* vol. II. New York: Harper and Row, 1963.

The following sources provide evidence of human attitudes toward the natural environment and the effects upon the earth of increasing human demands.

Anderson, Walt. *Politics and Environment: A Reader in the Ecological Crisis.* Pacific Palisades, California: Goodyear Publishing Co., 1970.

Cicero. *Tusculan Disputations; Also Treatises on the Nature of the Gods and on the Commonwealth.* Literally translated from the Latin, chiefly by Yonge, C.D. New York: Harper and Brothers, 1894.

Darby, H.C. "The Clearing of the Woodland in Europe," in Thomas, William L., Jr. *Man's Role in Changing the Face of the Earth,* vol. I. Chicago: University of Chicago Press, 1950.

Glasken, Clarence J. "Changing Ideas in a Habitable World," in Thomas, William L., Jr. *Man's Role in Changing the Face of the Earth*, vol. I. Chicago: University of Chicago Press, 1970.

Mencius. *The Four Books: Confucian Analects, The Great Learning, The Doctrine of the Mean, and the Works*. Translated from the Chinese with notes by James Legge. Shanghai: Chenein Book Company, 1933, vi.1.8.

Narr, Karl J. "Early Food Producing Populations" in Thomas, William L., Jr. *Man's Role in Changing the Face of the Earth*, vol. I. Chicago: University of Chicago Press, 1970.

Chapter 4

Basic questions about human competition, conflict, aggression, and mutual assistance can be derived from

Choucri, Nazli, and Robert C. North. *Nations in Conflict*. San Francisco, W.H. Freeman, 1975.

Gorney, Roderic. "Interpersonal Intensity, Competition, and Synergy Determinants of Achievement, Aggression, and Mental Illness," *American Journal of Psychiatry* (October 1971), vol. 128, no. 4.

Gladstone, Arthur. "Relationship Orientation and the Processes Leading Toward War," *Background* (1962), vol. 6.

Maslow, Abraham, "Synergy in the Society and Individual," *Journal of Individual Psychology* (1964), 20:153-64.

Richardson, Lewis F. *Arms and Insecurity*. Pittsburgh and Chicago: The Boxwood Press and Quadrangle Books, Inc., 1960.

Singer, J. David. "The Political Science of Human Conflict," in McNeil, Elton B. *The Nature of Human Conflict*. Englewood Cliffs, New Jersey: Prentice-Hall, 1965.

Styler, George S. "Competition," *International Encyclopaedia of the Social Sciences*. Second Edition, p. 181. New York: Macmillan, 1968.

von Bertalanffy, Ludwig. *General System Theory*. New York: George Braziller, 1968.

Chapter 5

Readings on social Darwinism, unrestrained competition, and notions of "survival of the fittest" include

Hofstadter, Richard. *Social Darwinism in American Thought*. Revised Edition. Boston: Beacon Press, 1955.

Nasmyth, George. *Social Progress and the Darwinian Theory: A Study of Force as a Factor in Human Relations*. New York: G.P. Putnam's Sons, 1916.

Spencer, Herbert. *Social Statistics*. New York: D. Appleton and Co., 1864.

Sumner, William Graham. *The Challenge of Facts and Other Essays*. New Haven: Yale University Press, 1914.

———. *What Social Classes Owe to Each Other*. New Haven: Yale University Press, 1925.

Tax, Sol, and Larry S. Krucoff. "Social Darwinism," *International Encyclopaedia of the Social Sciences*. Second Edition, vol. 14, p. 403. New York: Macmillan, 1968.

Ward, Lester F. "Evolution of Social Structures," *American Journal of Sociology* (March 1905), vol. X, no. 3.

The following sources will suggest some of the basic assumptions and propositions associated with competition-welfare concepts of society.

Galbraith, John Kenneth. *American Capitalism*. Boston: Houghton Mifflin, 1952.

———. *Beyond the Marshall Plan*. National Planning Association, Pamphlet No. 67

(February 1949).

MacPherson, C.B. *Democratic Theory: Essays in Retrieval.* Oxford: Clarendon Press, 1973.

Rawls, John. *A Theory of Justice.* Cambridge: Harvard University Press, 1971.

Smith, Adam. *An Inquiry into the Nature and Causes of the Wealth of Nations,* vol. II. London: W. Strahan and T. Cadell, 1776.

Wallich, Henry C. *The Cost of Freedom: A New Look at Capitalism.* New York: Harper Bros., 1960.

Sources for the multilevel, equal-access model are difficult to find. Anarchist writers of the nineteenth and early twentieth centuries provide a considerable number of applicable concepts, but those sources were not used in this book. In addition to ethnographic sources such as those drawn upon in Chapter 2, the reader might consult

Hignett, C. *A History of the Athenian Constitution to the End of the Fifth Century B.C.* Oxford: Clarendon Press, 1952.

Lasswell, Harold D., and Abraham Kaplan. *Power and Society.* New Haven, Yale University Press, 1950.

Chapter 6

Some important links between population, technology, resources, and the physical environment can be inferred from

Bennett, John W. *The Ecological Transition: Cultural Anthropology and Human Adaptation.* New York: Pergamon Press, 1976.

North, Robert C., and Nazli Choucri. "Population and the International System: Some Implications for United States Policy and Planning," in A.E. Keir Nash. *Governance and Population: The Governmental Implications of Population Change.* The Commission on Population Growth and the American Future. Washington: Government Printing Office, 1972, vol. IV.

Odum, Howard T. *Environment, Power and Society.* New York: Wiley-Interscience, 1971.

Chapter 7

The reader concerned with basic human motivations and incentives—together with their implications for social, economic, and political organization—will find two titles especially useful.

Lasswell, Harold. *Politics: Who Gets What, When, How.* New York: Meridian Books, 1958.

Maslow, Abraham. *Motivation and Personality.* New York: Harper and Row, 1970.

The question of who wins and who loses in the world's economic system today is discussed by

Galbraith, J. Kenneth. *Economics and the Public Purpose.* New York: Signet, 1975.

Analyses of the relationships between human values and economic development are provided by

Goulet, Denis. *The Cruel Choice.* New York: Atheneum, 1973.

LeGuin, Ursula. *The Dispossessed.* New York: Harper and Row, 1974.

Other titles dealing with problems of economic growth, competitions, and maldistributions include

Brown, Lester R. "The Interdependence of Nations." *Headline Series* No. 212. New York: Foreign Policy Association, October 1972.

Hodson, H.V. *The Diseconomies of Growth.* New York: Ballantine Books, 1972.

Thompson, William Irwin. *Passages About Earth*. New York: Harper and Row, 1973.

For empirical data on relationships between technological growth and basic quality of life indicators I am personally indebted to

Goldstein, Joshua. "World Industrialization and the Quality of Life," an unpublished paper. Department of Political Science, Stanford University, California.

A convenient, non-polemical source book for empirical data on world social indicators and arms expenditures—referred to recently as "a statistical analytical report on where the world's wealth goes" and "a devastating indictment against the human race"—has been published recently by an economist, who allows numbers to speak for values with a minimum of verbal comment.

Sivard, Ruth Leger. *World Military and Social Expenditures, 1976*. Leesburg, Va.: WMSE Publications, 1976.

I have argued that every increase in human demands, often rationalized in terms of "needs," increases our dependence upon forces that are difficult, if not impossible, to control. A contemporary economist's practical, as well as theoretical, approach to this issue is presented by

Schumacher, E.F. *Small Is Beautiful: Economics as if People Mattered*. New York: Torchbooks, 1973.

A concise prescription for Britain's survival today—a prescription with implications for other countries of the world as well—can be found in

Editors of the Ecologist: Edward Goldsmith and others. *Blueprint for Survival*. Boston: Houghton Mifflin, 1972.

A British economist's criticism of the world's "remarkable faith in the ultimate beneficence" of industrial growth is presented in

Mishan, E.F. *Technology and Growth: The Price We Pay*. New York: Praeger, 1970.

An excellent collection of short essays by leading social scientists who doubt that economic and industrial growth can continue at current rates without severe cost to humankind is contained in

Daly, Herman E. *Toward a Steady-State Economy*. San Francisco: W.H. Freeman, 1973.

The first popularized presentation of global dynamics using computer-based simulated models and depicting world growth trends in terms of population, technology, energy and other resource use, food production, and food consumption was the first Club of Rome report presented by

Meadows, Donella and Dennis. *The Limits to Growth*. New York: Signet, 1972.

The second Club of Rome report, which made the case for an integrated world system based on mutual dependence, was prepared by

Mesarovic, M., and E. Pestel. *Mankind at the Turning Point*. New York: E.P. Dutton, 1974.

The Institute for World Order, 1140 Avenue of the Americas, New York, N.Y. 10036, carries on a broad program of education and policy research with respect to the global future. Publications include *Transition*, which appears bi-monthly, and a book series which includes

Beres, Louis René, and Harry Targ. *Reordering the Planet*. Boston: Allyn and Bacon, 1973.

Falk, Richard A. *A Study of Future Worlds*. New York: Free Press, 1975.

———. *A Global Approach to National Policy*. Cambridge. Harvard University Press, 1975.

Kothari, Rajni. *Footsteps into the Future*. New York: Free Press, 1974.

Laslo, Erwin. *A Strategy for the Future*. New York: Braziller, 1974.

Mendelovitz, Saul, ed. *On the Creation of a Just World Order*. New York: Free Press, 1975.

Also helpful for those who would like to participate in the design of alternate futures are

Bernstein, Paul. *Workplace Democratization: Its Internal Dynamics*. Kent, Ohio: Kent State University Press, 1976.

Elgin, Duane S., David C. MacMichael, and Peter Schwartz. *Alternative Futures for Environmental Planning*. Washington, D.C.: Environmental Protection Agency, 5401, 9-75-027.

Falk, Richard A. "Future Worlds," *Headline Series* No. 229. New York: Foreign Policy Association, February 1976.

Wager, W. Warren. *Building the City of Man*. New York: Grossman, 1971.

In dealing with problems of relating utopias to environments, I am grateful to the following authors for having been given the opportunity to read a preliminary draft of their book manuscript.

Moos, Rudolf and Robert Brownstein. *Environment and Utopia*. New York: Plenum, 1977.

For insights into the possible use of existing international institutions as models for non-coercive approaches to many world and national regulatory problems, I am indebted to a veteran international civil servant recently turned academic.

Wallenstein, Gerd D. "Collaboration Without Coercion: An Organizational Model for International Standardization," a doctoral dissertation, Stanford University, 1976.

Among general discussions of contemporary model-building, the following offer useful starting points.

Choucri, Nazli, and Thomas Robinson. *Forecasting and International Relations: Theory, Methods, Problems, Prospects*. San Francisco: W.H. Freeman, in press.

Jantsch, Erich. *Technological Planning and Social Futures*. London: Associated Business Programmes, Ltd., 1972.

Lave, Charles A., and James G. March. *An Introduction to Models in the Social Sciences*. New York: Harper and Row, 1975. (For the would-be modeler, *this is where to begin.*)

Mayr, Otto. *The Origins of Feedback Control*. Cambridge: MIT Press, 1969.

Platt, John. "How Men Can Shape Their Futures," *Futures* (March 1971).

Powers, William T. *Behavior: The Control of Perception*. Chicago: Aldine Publishing Co., 1973. (This is an extremely important book.)

Weiner, Norbert. *The Human Use of Human Beings*. Boston: Houghton Mifflin, 1950.

The optimistic and pessimistic projections are modified from a contribution of mine to

Wallia, C.S. *Toward Century 21*. New York: Basic Books, 1970.

Additional information about PLATO can be obtained from

Handler, Paul. *Programmed Logic for Automatic Teaching Operation*, Population Dynamics Group. University of Illinois, Urbana, Illinois.

ABOUT THE AUTHOR

After graduating in 1936 from Union College with a major in language and literature, Robert North became a travel lecturer for several years, taking 16mm. movies in Latin America, northern Scandinavia, the Central Sahara, and other parts of the world. During World War II he served as air-ground liaison officer with army amphibious assault battalions in the Central and South Pacific and in the Philippines, acquiring seven battle stars. After the war he took his AM in international relations and his PhD in political science, both at Stanford University. Before joining the Political Science Department in 1957 (where he has been a full professor since 1962), he was on the Hoover Institution staff for ten years, first as research assistant and later as research associate. During the late 1940s and early 1950s his research and teaching focused largely on Sino-Soviet relations. Since then, he has been concerned with the antecedents of war, the behavior of states and empires, and worldwide trends in population, technology, and access to resources. In recent years he has participated in an interdisciplinary, team-taught course which brings perspectives from engineering, economics, anthropology, political science, and education to bear upon contemporary problems of population growth, applications of technology, resource allocations, and organized violence. His publications include *Moscow and Chinese Communists* (1962), *Soviet Russia and the East* (1956), of which he is co-author, and *Nations in Conflict* (1975), also co-authored. In 1969-70 he served as president of the International Studies Association.

Index

INDEX